I0600429

AN AMISH CHRISTMAS BLESSING

PATRICK E. CRAIG

PUBLISHING

PRAISE FOR PATRICK E. CRAIG'S BOOKS

An Amish Christmas Blessing. Wow, you are in for an amazing read with this book, it's a dual time slip read packed full of history, family, community and faith. As I was reading I realized that this genre may be one of my favorite kinds of book. It's like being immersed into a family throughout generations of trials, blessings and love.

— **CHERESE AKHAVEIN** - REVIEWER

"I haven't cried like this in a while. *When The Hummingbirds Danced In A Honeysuckle Sky* is a stark examen of redemption. With unfiltered beauty, Patrick Craig draws the darkest of masculine and feminine trauma to the impossible, hoped for light of undeserved, tender, most patient love. To give, without thought of return, to sacrifice without reserve, and constancy, this is what you'll find in Craig's muscular narrative of what it means to be saved... from oneself. "

— **ANN MALLEY,** AUTHOR OF THE DIAMOND DOG SERIES

I would certainly recommend *When the Hummingbirds Danced in a Honeysuckle Sky* as a poignant exploration of reconciliation and legacy that is perfectly paced and powerfully told.

— **K.C. FINN,** FIVE STAR REVIEW — READER'S FAVORITE

Patrick E. Craig has once again written a book that will take you deep into the heart of Amish country. *The Quilt That Knew* is a delightful and intriguing plain and simple mystery.

— **VANNETTA CHAPMAN**, USA TODAY
BESTSELLING AUTHOR

I have over 500 books on my Kindle, but only nine books are listed under "Favorite Christian Books". Three of those nine are the *Apple Creek Dreams Series.* The characters are believable, lovable, flawed human beings.

— **AMAZON READER**

For my Grandmother, Nettie Patrick Craig, whose picture sits on my writing desk and whose family fame as a true Irish shanachie has inspired me in my writing journey for many years.

ACKNOWLEDGMENTS

To all my readers, old and new, who encourage me to continue on
this writing path.

Cover by Cora Graphics Simona Cora Salardi

www.coragraphics.it

An Amish Christmas Blessing

Copyright © 2025 by Patrick E. Craig

Published by P&J Publishing

P.O. Box 73

Huston, Idaho 83630

Library of Congress Cataloging-in-publications Data

Craig, Patrick E., 1947-

An Amish Christmas Blessing / Patrick E. Craig

ISBN 979-8-9937031-1-4 (pbk.)

ISBN 979-8-9937031-0-7 (eBook)

Printed in the United States of America

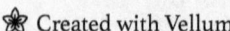 Created with Vellum

A NOTE FROM PATRICK E. CRAIG

I wrote The Amish Menorah as a standalone story almost seven years ago. Elk Lake Publishers included it in *The Amish Menorah and Other Stories*, an anthology put together by several men who write in the Amish fiction genre. *The Amish Menorah* introduced my readers to Gerd Hirschberg, an Amish farmer in the Rhineland during the tumultuous years of the Nazi rise to power in the late 1930s, and Emily Weissbach, a Jewish girl Gerd found hiding in his barn, and their adventures escaping from the Nazis. Then a few years after, I wrote another story, *A Light in the Window*, based on the life of Gerd and Emily Hirschberg after they came to America. I contributed the story to a different anthology of Amish stories, *A Christmas Collection*, but I have always wanted to weave the two stories together. So now I am giving my readers *An Amish Christmas Blessing* and introducing a fourth-generation member of the family, Abigail Harris. In the story of Abigail's awakening to her heritage, both in the Amish community and the Jewish faith, and finally to a family heritage of faith in Christ, I am including the two stories I wrote previously. I am doing this hoping the story of Gerd and Emily and their descendants will reach a wider audience. So, enjoy, and may this book be a blessing.

Patrick E. Craig

Chapter One

THE VISITORS

*a*bigail Harris woke from her nap. It was hot in the Volkswagen. She felt grungy and sweaty. They had been on the road for two days, on their way to upstate New York to a friend's house. Now, because of some bad luck, they had taken a detour to Colorado.

The trip came into being a week earlier in L.A., when Tommy Martin, her boyfriend, came home from one of his 'meetings.' He flung himself down on the couch in the 'living room' of his mother's basement where they were living, put his hands behind his head, and stretched out.

"Pack your gear, Abby. We are blowing this popsicle stand."

"What?"

"Yeah. I need to meet some friends in New York. There are big things about to happen, and I don't want to miss out."

"Well, how long will we be gone, Tommy?"

Tommy shrugged and grinned. "I don't know. A while."

"But what about my job?" She could see the anger flare up on his face.

"Always about you, isn't it, Abby?"

"But..."

"Forget your job. There are a lot more important things to worry about than your job."

"But it's the only source of income we have. You're not working, and…"

"Gonna throw that in my face again? Don't you see that I have important work to do? I can't get all hung up working nine to five. That's not who I am. After this trip, I'm gonna be important."

"Well, how are we going to pay for this… trip?"

"You've got some money in the bank. We'll use that."

"But that's all I… we… have."

Tommy stood up. "Don't throw excuses at me. How much do we have?"

"About two thousand dollars."

"Good. That should get us there with plenty to spare."

"But what do we do if it runs out?"

"Leave that to me. I have some connections in New York, and I can scam some money from them. So, don't worry. It won't run out."

It did.

———

THE CAR BROKE down in Albuquerque. They barely made it to a gas station outside of town. The man who worked there promised he could fix Volkswagens. He couldn't. They spent three hours at the Denny's across the street and $1,700 at the parts window. They got in the car and sat. Tommy was angry.

"I never should have bought this hunk of junk."

Abigail looked at Tommy, then looked away.

You didn't buy it; I did. You just registered it in your name.

"So, what are we going to do now, Tommy?"

Tommy scowled. "Just cool your jets, I'm thinking." He sat for a minute. "Say, didn't you say you have relatives in Colorado?"

Abigail nodded. "Yes, a great-uncle, my grandmother's brother."

"What was the town?"

"Grandma Adina told me she grew up near a town called Alamosa."

Tommy nodded. "Hand me that map."

Abigail dug in the door pocket and brought out the map. Tommy pulled it out of her hands and spread it out. "Okay, we are in Albuquerque." He put his finger on the map and traced a line north. "Here it is, Alamosa, Colorado. And guess what? It's only about two hundred miles north of here. That's only four hours. We'll go there, and you can borrow some cash."

"But, Tommy, I've never met Uncle Jürgen. I can't just go barging in there and ask for money."

Tommy looked up. "You can, and you will. We have one hundred and fifty dollars left. That won't even get us to Kansas City. If you can borrow three or four hundred, we'll have just about enough."

"But, Tommy..."

"Be quiet, Abby. Just start thinking about how you're going to sweet-talk the old geezer. You know, use your feminine wiles, all that stuff."

Abigail didn't like it, but it seemed like their only hope.

JÜRGEN HIRSCHBERG HEARD the car before he saw it.

Timing's off; it's missing badly, one of them little German cars...

He watched as the Volkswagen Bug crawled around the corner of the barn and into the barnyard. It jerked to a stop and sat for a minute. Then two people emerged—one, the driver, a young, scrawny-looking man with longish hair and a scowl, and the other, a pretty young blonde. The blonde spoke first.

"Mr. Hirschberg?"

"Yes?"

"I'm Abigail Harris."

"That should mean something to me?"

"I'm Yvette Harris's daughter."

"And?"

"Yvette was Adina's daughter."

"My sister, Adina?"

"Yes."

"What are you doing here?"

Jürgen noted the surprised look on the girl's face.

"Well, I'm your niece, uh, great-niece…"

"And you're expecting a parade, maybe?"

"But, Mr. Hirschberg…"

"What?"

"Well, I'm your niece, and I was hoping you might…"

Jürgen shook his head. "Look, I'm a busy man. I'm getting ready to go to work and a woman who claims to be my niece, a woman I've never met or even seen a picture of, a woman accompanied by a scruffy-looking hippie, this woman drives into my yard, and I'm supposed to kill the fatted calf. Gather around the campfire and sing 'Kum Bayh Yah'? I don't think so. Now, state your business and then get on down the road. I've got work to do."

The young man took a half-step forward. "Why you, you can't…"

Jürgen just looked at him. "Finish that step and what you are about to say, and it may be something you will regret for a while." He turned back to the girl. "Now! State your business and then get off my place."

The young man scowled again, but his mouth stayed shut, and he didn't move.

The girl walked around the car and took hold of the young man's arm. "Let me speak to him, Tommy." She turned back to Jürgen. "We are here because we need your help. We have been traveling across the country, and our car broke down. Getting it fixed took most of our traveling money..."

"You got cheated."

"Excuse me?"

Jürgen pointed at the car. "If you spent money and the 'fixer' claimed he fixed it, you got cheated. The timing is way off, and I can tell by the little blue puff of smoke from the exhaust you pumped out when you downshifted, the engine rings are bad. What made you think you could get across the country in this pile of junk?"

The kid spoke up. "I don't have to listen to this stuff. What does he know about...?"

This time Jürgen walked right over and stood above the young man, who cowered back. "What is there about keep quiet or I'll throw you bodily off my place that you don't understand?"

The girl interposed herself between the two men. "Please, Mr. Hirschberg, I'm sorry. Tommy won't say anything more, will you?" She gave Tommy a hard look. Tommy lowered his eyes. "No."

"In fact, Tommy, why don't you sit in the car while I talk to my uncle." Tommy looked at her and then at Jürgen, who towered at least five inches above him. He turned and climbed back into the car.

"Now, Uncle Jürgen..."

"Mr. Hirschberg will do."

The girl blushed. "I'm sorry... Mr. Hirschberg. I really am your niece. I can show you my birth certificate and tell you everything you need to know about my mother and some about my grandmother, Adina."

Jürgen shook his head. "Look, young lady, what you say may be true; you may be my niece, but I don't know you from Eve. Around here, we judge a person by the company they keep and the gut feel you get when you meet 'em. So far, you've failed."

"Okay, I understand we didn't make a good first impression..."

Jürgen chuckled. "An understatement."

"Okay, I haven't gotten off on the right foot, but as of now you are my only hope. I'm... we're in trouble and we need your help."

"So, you hoped you could gin up some family connection and hit me up for something. Money, no doubt."

The young woman took a deep breath. "You're right. I'll get right to the point. Tommy and I are going to see some friends in upstate New York. Our car broke down. The repairs were expensive, and they took most of our money. If you could just help us— well... help me—maybe loan me a few hundred dollars, enough to get to New York, I promise I will pay it back as soon as I get there."

Jürgen laughed. "Young lady, I may have been born at night, but I wasn't born last night." He saw the crestfallen look on Abigail's face. "So, you thought that blood might be thicker than water. Just because you have some obscure family claim, I'm supposed to reach in my pocket and hand you some money? That's not how life works." Then Jürgen saw the tears on her face. He thought for a moment and then took a deep breath. "Stay here. I'll be back in a minute." Jürgen walked several steps away and stood looking at the sky for several minutes. He nodded and then he turned and walked back. He looked at the disheveled girl standing in front of him for a long time. Then he spoke.

"Okay, tell you what. I got some chores that need doin' around here. I'll let you stay for three days and work. I'll feed you and give you a place to stay. If you do a good job, I'll pay you each one hundred and fifty dollars. Then you can go on your merry way. What say you?"

Abigail's face brightened. "That would be fine, Uncle... Mr. Hirschberg." She turned to the car. "Tommy, Tommy, Mr. Hirschberg has offered to pay us if we do some work for him."

Tommy's door opened, and he stuck his head out. "What kind of work? Does it have anything to do with cows?"

"Horses, Mr. Tommy. We raise horses here." Jürgen pointed to the barn. "If you go in there, you will find a row of thirty stalls. All of them need to be mucked out."

"What's mucked out?"

Jürgen walked to a shed a few feet away. He opened the door, went inside, and began bringing out tools. When he finished, there were two pitchforks, two shovels, two brooms and a wheelbarrow.

"Mucking out stalls is how I keep my barn clean. Very simple. First, you scoop out the manure and the soiled straw they sleep on. Put it in the wheelbarrow and take it out to the manure pile behind the barn. Replace the bedding and sweep the surrounding area. Takes about an hour a stall. Figure three days will be plenty for the two of you to get the barn done. You can start in the morning."

Tommy looked around. "So where do we sleep?"

"You two married?"

Abigail turned a light shade of red. She looked down. "No."

Jürgen pointed to the girl. "I've got a spare bedroom upstairs for you." He pointed at Tommy. "You'll sleep out here."

Tommy bristled. "Wait a minute, we live together. You can't tell us..."

Jürgen raised his hand. "You may live together in your house, but not mine. That's the way it is. My house, my rules. Take it or leave it."

Tommy glared at Jürgen and then at Abigail. "You gonna let him tell us we can't sleep together?"

Abigail shrugged. "It seems like we don't have a choice."

"There's a cot with blankets in the bunk room at the end of the barn. Toilet, sink, shower, everything you'll need."

"What about food?"

"I said I'd feed you, didn't I? Soup's on the menu. I eat at five o'clock sharp in the kitchen. And I mean sharp."

AT 5:15, Tommy Martin strolled into the kitchen. There were no pots on the stove, and Jürgen and Abigail were finishing a bowl of soup.

"Hey, sorry I'm late. I fell asleep in the car. Where's the soup?"

Jürgen looked up. "I said sharp. The soup's put away. Come back for breakfast. 5:30 a.m."

Tommy looked at the old man, his mouth open. "As in 5:30 in the morning?"

"Any other 5:30 a.m.?"

"But I'm hungry now. Gimme some of that bread." He reached for the loaf of shepherd's bread on a cutting board by Jürgen. Suddenly, a steel grip immobilized his arm.

Jürgen rose and took Tommy by the coat front. "Look, kid, I don't like you. I don't like people who go into another man's house without so much as a 'by-your-leave' and try to take things. Now when I say you can stay and work, I'm only doin' it because your girlfriend was upset, and she seems like a nice young lady. But you? You kinda put me off my feed. So, if you want to make some traveling money, you'll follow my rules. If you do that, I'll feed you and give you a place to sleep for the next three days. Then you can be on your merry way. Is that understood? Just nod."

Tommy nodded.

"That means breakfast is at 5:30. Folks who show at 5:31 don't eat. Understood? Just nod."

Tommy nodded again.

"Good, we understand each other. So now, since I don't have a TV, there's nothing more for you here. If I was you, I'd go bed down and get some shut-eye. 4:30 comes awfully early in the San Luis Valley."

"4:30? But I thought you said 5:30?"

"Well, you better get up at 4:30 so you can make yourself presentable before you show up on time at my table by 5:30. Presentable as in showered and shaved. Understood? Just nod."

Tommy nodded.

Jürgen released him. "Good night, Mr. Tommy."

Tommy turned and walked through the door, glaring at Abigail as he left.

Abigail, who sat silently through the exchange with Tommy, watched him go and then spoke up. "Really, Mr. Hirschberg, Tommy is a nice guy when you get to know him. Why he's very intelligent and knows all kinds of things."

Jürgen smiled. "He may be intelligent, but he's not very smart. And you say he knows all kinds of things. But he's kinda sparse on the basics. You know, things like showing up on time, looking like he cares about the way he looks, being respectful to his elders, honoring you as a woman, and not trying to push someone around who's doing him a favor."

"But he has a degree from Cal Poly. In Political Science."

"Got him a good job, did it?"

"Well, he's very busy with writing, and speaking at different meetings."

"Does he get paid?"

"Well, no, but he has a higher calling. He wants to educate the masses, show them how to better themselves, break the yoke of tyranny the elite class shoved down our throats for the last two hundred years."

Jürgen laughed out loud. "Break the yoke of tyranny. Why, he sounds like a dang Bolshevik. And let me tell you something. That boy couldn't show anybody how to break a pencil with both hands." He laughed again. "Come on, girl. I'll show you to your room."

Chapter Two

ABANDONED

*A*bigail came down to breakfast at 5:20 a.m. The smell of bacon filled the kitchen. There was a plate of hotcakes on the table and some eggs cooking in a pan on the stove. Jürgen was tending them, dressed and ready for the day. "Came a little early to make sure your boyfriend made it to breakfast?"

Abigail blushed. "Well, I..."

"He ain't gonna make it."

"What do you mean?"

"He left in the night, soon as you went to bed. Pushed the car around to the other side of the barn so you wouldn't hear it start up and took off."

"What!" Abigail ran out the back door and into the barnyard. Jürgen was right. The car was gone. A horrible sinking feeling filled her. Then she felt a hand on her shoulder. It was Jürgen.

"Come on back and have some breakfast. You'll feel better... and then we'll talk."

Abigail went back inside with the old man. She didn't think she could eat, but surprisingly, the smell of the bacon and the sight of the pancakes and eggs overwhelmed her upset, and she soon was eating heartily.

Jürgen smiled at the empty plate. "Sufficient unto the day is the evil thereof."

"What?"

"It's just something Jesus used to say. It means, don't worry about tomorrow since today is bad enough. Like some coffee?"

"Oh, please!"

Jürgen poured her a cup and offered her cream. She nodded yes, noticing that he took his black. Jürgen motioned toward the doorway into the front room. "Come on, let's sit in the living room. I want to talk to you for a minute."

They went to the living room. A roaring blaze in the fireplace felt wonderful to Abigail. Jürgen pointed her to the couch and then sat in a chair across from her.

"What will you do?"

Abigail put her coffee down on an end table, sat for a moment, and then put her face in her hands. She whispered. "I don't know, Mr. Hirschberg, I don't know."

"Caught between a rock and a hard place, ain't ya?"

Sniffles. "Apparently."

"Didn't you know he would bail on you if push came to shove?"

"He told me he loved me. That we would change the world together."

"But he got you into his bed without marrying you and left when the horse dung hit the fan. You been suckered, gal."

"Seems so, doesn't it?"

"Got no relatives to go to?"

"My mom died three years ago in a car accident. My dad left me with his parents and went to Venezuela to work in the oil fields. An explosion on an oil derrick killed him, too. As you know, Grandmother Adina died several years ago, right after her husband, Grandpa Thompson, died."

"Yeah, I heard." Jürgen paused, then went on. "What about your dad's parents?"

"After Dad died, I moved in with Tommy. We had a room in his mother's house. Then, Grandpa Harris had a stroke, and Grandma couldn't take care of him, so they sold their house and moved him into assisted living. She lives there with him, so there is no place to go back to."

"Stuck with Mr. Tommy, eh?"

Abigail nodded.

"Lived off his mom, didn't have a job, while you waited tables or something?"

"I worked at a bookstore. How did you know?"

"Men like Mr. Tommy are easy to read. I been in the horse business all my life. Horse traders are a microcosm of all humanity. My papa taught me human nature, how to read people. It's essential if you don't want to get cheated. You see, men fall into two categories. They either tell the truth or they're four-flushers."

"What's that?"

"A low-down dirty dog, a cheat, a fraud, someone who tries to bluff other people. I knew right away Mr. Tommy was a con man."

"But how?"

"Well, for one thing, he thought he was the smartest guy in the room. He tried to bluff me, but he was a coward. He backed off and let you do the talking. A real man would have protected you and presented your case, but he let you present his. He was also disrespectful. He showed up late for dinner and then thought I owed him something to eat. I could see right away that he was the most important person in his life, not you. Only took him three hours to prove it. Did he have a credit card?"

"Maybe, but he never told me."

"A guy like him always has a backup plan. He probably stole it from his mother when you left. He's been living off the money you had in your savings, right? Letting you spend your money?"

Abigail nodded.

"He'll use the card to get to New York before his mother can cancel it. Before she does, he'll draw some cash. Then he'll buy a bunch of food for the trip. And wine... he's a wine man, right?"

Abigail looked at Jürgen. "How do you know all this stuff?"

Jürgen chuckled. "A man my age has been around the corral a few times. Reading people like Mr. Tommy comes with the territory."

Abigail sighed. "I guess I was pretty foolish."

Jürgen nodded. "I'd say so. But that doesn't mean there ain't a remedy."

"What do you mean, Mr. Hirschberg?"

"Well, I kinda like you, and since we are kin, I got a proposition. I thought about it some last night, prayed about it, and I reckon I got my answer."

"What do you mean, Mr. Hirschberg?"

"Well, my offer to work still stands. If you want to do chores around here for room and board, I'll let you do that. 'Course I won't work you as hard as my hired hand, but it'll be ranch work for sure. And I have some friends in town who own a restaurant. We could see about getting you a paying job. If we do, there's a bus runs by here every morning and every night that would take you into town and bring you back. How does that sound?"

Abigail looked at Jürgen. Despite his gruff demeanor, his eyes were kind.

"I don't know how to thank you."

"Well, all right then. Now if you look in the closet in the room I put you in, you will find some jeans and a warm shirt. They were Adina's when she was very young, and they ought to fit you. Then I'll show you around the place and we'll get to work."

ABIGAIL GAVE herself a quick glance in the mirror. The shirt and pants fit her almost perfectly.

I look almost like a Western girl.

She glanced down at her manicured hands.

And I suppose my fingernails will look Western soon enough...

She sighed and started to go out, and then she realized something. She didn't miss Tommy. In fact, she felt like a load had gone off her shoulders.

That's odd. I thought I loved him.

Another thought.

How did I let him sweet-talk me into going with him?

She saw a stretchable hair band on the dresser, so she pulled her hair back into a ponytail and wrapped the band around it. Then she headed for the stairs. Jürgen was waiting by the kitchen door. He handed her a pair of gloves.

"There's some of my mom's old muck boots out on the mud porch. They should fit."

They headed out to the barn. Jürgen gave her the mucking tools, gave her a few instructions, and then headed off to see about some horses in a back pasture. Abigail looked at the mess in the first stall, sighed and then started in. After about half an hour of scooping and shoveling, she had made little progress in her first stall, and her back was hurting.

"There's a better way to do that."

Abigail jumped and whirled around. A tall, good-looking young man in overalls and a flat hat stood by the door smiling at her.

"Oh, my goodness, you scared me silly."

The young man smiled. "Sorry about that. Didn't mean to sneak up on you."

"I thought my heart would stop. That was mean."

"Well, I saw you going at that stall and I thought maybe you'd like some help."

Abigail lifted her nose and sniffed. "I'm doing just fine."

The young man smiled again. "Not really."

Abigail felt her hackles rise. "Say, what makes you the expert?"

"Don't get your dander up. I'm Johan Eicher. I work for Mr. Hirschberg. I've mucked out ten thousand stalls if I've mucked out one. If you're willing to accept some help..."

Something about this young man got under Abigail's skin. "You must have some other work to do." She turned back to the unmanageable mess in the stall... and had an epiphany. She turned around just as Johan was going out the door.

"Wait. I'm sorry. I... I guess I need some help."

Johan stuck his head back in the door, a smile on his face. "You sure? Don't want to spoil your fun."

Abigail dropped her head. "I'm willing to take a few pointers, if you would be so kind."

Johan walked back into the barn. He picked up the shovel. "Okay. First, pick out the large, obvious big manure piles and wet spots." He scooped the worst heaps of manure efficiently into the wheelbarrow. "Starting at the door, move around the stall in a circle. Sort the bedding as you go. Toss what's clean enough to keep along the walls or into corners. Pile the soiled stuff in the center." He showed how to do it. "Now grab the fork. Make a circuit or two, doing the same thing, then scoop out the soiled bedding in the pile you've made in just a few forkfuls. Put it in the wheelbarrow." Again, Johan demonstrated. His movements were smooth, nothing wasted, his brow knit in concentration. "Pull the reserved bedding that you put along the walls into the center of the stall." He walked along the walls, forking the usable bedding into a layer in the center of the stall. "If what's there is too thin, you can add a layer of new clean. It's right over there in a pile." He walked over, got a forkful of straw, and added it to the layer on the floor of the stall. "And that's it. Doing it that way will save you about twenty-five minutes a stall. It adds up."

Abigail looked at the stall in amazement. In about twenty minutes, Johan had turned the stall from a mess into a comfortable place for a horse to sleep.

Abigail realized she had been a little snarky. She looked up at

Johan. "Thank you. That is extremely helpful." She lowered her eyes, felt the blush steal up her face. "I'm sorry I was a little short with you." She looked up at him.

Johan smiled, and Abigail noticed that even though he and Tommy were about the same age, Johan's smile was manly and grown up, not the silly, vacuous grin that Tommy often wore, especially when he was drinking. She stuffed her thoughts back and asked a question.

"That's not a Western hat, is it?"

Johan shook his head. "No, it's an Amish hat. I'm Amish. I live over in Monte Vista. There's an Amish community there."

"I don't know much about the Amish."

Johan smiled again. "Ask Jürgen. He's Amish too... in his own way. Well, I've got my work." He turned to go.

"Thank you again, Johan. It was very kind of you."

Johan touched his hat brim. "Glad to help."

Abigail watched him go.

A different guy than Tommy, that's for sure.

Chapter Three

HERITAGE

*A*round noon, Jürgen came to the barn. He looked at Abigail's clean stalls and nodded. Following Johan's instructions, she had worked her way through five of them. She had not done it as quickly as Johan, but his method was certainly an improvement on the way she had been approaching the task.

"Good job, Abigail. You took to this like a duck to water."

She shook her head. "Well, I had a little help."

"Ah, did Johan come by and show you his way?"

"Yes, and it really helped. I must admit, I was struggling."

"Well, he's a good lad."

"He's Amish?"

Jürgen nodded. "Yep, but for that matter, so am I... well, in my own way, I guess." He grinned.

"That's what Johan said. How do you mean, Mr. Hirschberg?"

"Well, my papa was Amish and his papa before him all the way back to the 1700s in Switzerland. My dad kinda didn't see eye-to-eye with the Amish though. Happened when he still lived in Germany and the Nazis hornswoggled the Amish in Germany into believing they were Aryan supermen because they were good farmers. They told them they were essential to the well-being of the Third Reich, so they went along with Hitler and his claptrap. Didn't sit well with my papa. But when he and my mother moved here from Germany, they got to know the Amish folks who live down the road in Monte Vista. He got along with them better. He brought his mother, his *mütti*, with him, and she fit right in. They all sat around yakkin' in High German. I like the Amish pretty good too, but I'm not a joiner."

"Does that make me Amish?"

"Well, now, I think you have to be raised under the *ordnüng*, the Amish rules for living, and get baptized into the church to be Amish. But I reckon you could convert. Anyway, it's in your bloodline for sure. And that's not all. You're also Jewish by descent."

"Jewish!"

"Sure. My mama was one hundred percent Jewish. The Jews trace their bloodlines through the mother. If your mother is Jewish, you are Jewish. So, me and Adina were Jewish by matrilineal descent, and the Jews considered your mother, Yvette, Jewish too, because Adina schooled her in the Jewish way that Emily, our mother, taught her. At least, that's what I heard. I got the same schooling, so the Jews around here accept me as one of their own. Now, those Jews might not consider you Jewish unless you was raised that way, but you sure got Jewish blood."

"So... I'm Amish and Jewish and I never knew a thing about it." Abigail's brow furrowed. "I'll have to think about that." She picked up her shovel. "Well, I guess I'll get back to my mucking."

Jürgen smiled. "Thought you might want a little lunch first. There's some sandwiches and soup."

"Oh, that would be wonderful. I guess I could use a break. Will... will Johan be there?"

"Sure. The hands eat with us on the ranch. Well, I must wash up. I'll see you up to the house."

When Abigail came into the kitchen, she was surprised to see a middle-aged woman making sandwiches at the kitchen counter. The woman wore a long, dark blue dress and a white cap set on the bun at the back of her head. The woman looked up and smiled. "*Guten tag!*" She noticed the puzzled look on Abigail's face. "That means good afternoon. You must be Abigail. Jürgen was telling me about you. I'm Maggie, Johan's mama."

"Are you... are you Amish, too?"

Maggie laughed, but it was a friendly laugh, and Abigail relaxed.

"I'm as Amish as you can get and then some. I do housekeeping for Jürgen a few days a week, and I try to keep him tapped into his Amish roots. His grandmother was a great addition to the Amish community when she came here in 1940. I remember her from when I was a very little girl. In fact, she brought about a kind of revival in our church."

Abigail's interest stirred. "Revival?"

"Yes, when *Mütti* came... *Mütti* was what everyone called her; it means mama or mommy in German. And that's what she was to all of us. She was a brilliant historian. She helped us to remember our German and Swiss roots, who we were, even though it was unpopular to be German in those days."

Maggie nodded at an empty chair and smiled. "*Setzen sie sich!*"

Abigail guessed that meant she could sit. She was about to ask more questions when the kitchen door opened and Jürgen and Johan came in. Jürgen looked at Abigail and then at Maggie. "She's schoolin' you in the ways of the Amish already? Ya gotta be careful with this lady. She can talk the hind leg off a mule."

Maggie raised the wooden spoon she had in her hand. "Why, you old coot. At least someone can hold a conversation around here. Talking to you is like talking to a grizzly bear. A person could die of loneliness with you sitting just across the table."

Jürgen nodded. "Careful. You'll get soup on your nice clean floor."

Johan smiled and sat down across from Abigail. He leaned forward and whispered. "Never mind these two. They talk like this, but I think they might actually like each other."

Maggie looked over. "Don't believe him, Abigail. There's not a word of truth in it. Now let's eat so you sluggards can get back to work."

She brought a plate full of sandwiches, set it on the table, and then brought the soup. Jürgen sat next to Abigail, and Maggie slid in next to her son. "Help yourself." Everyone dug in, filling their bowls, and taking a sandwich. Abigail was about to start when she saw Jürgen take Maggie's hand, and Johan did the same. Johan reached across, and Abigail slipped her hand into his while Jürgen took the other. Johan's hand was strong and warm, and a little thrill went through Abigail.

Good grief, girl. Your boyfriend just dumped you, and you're getting a thrill from a guy you don't even know. Sheesh!

Jürgen bowed his head. "Dear Heavenly Father. Enable us to use Thy manifold blessings with moderation; grant our hearts wisdom to avoid excess in eating and drinking and in the cares of this life; teach us to put our trust in Thee and to await Thy helping hand. Amen."

Maggie and Johan said 'Amen' and Abigail, caught by surprise, echoed them but a split second behind them. She felt her face flush.

Now why would that make me upset? I didn't know they were going to pray.

Maggie looked over at Abigail. "Since you're staying for a bit, you should have Jürgen fill you in on your family history."

Jürgen turned to Maggie. "Now, Maggie, what if Abigail isn't interested?"

Abigail perked up. "Oh, but I am, especially since finding out my family's background has raised a few questions for me."

Maggie smiled. "I'm sure."

Johan grinned. "Quite a surprise for you, no doubt."

Abigail looked down. "My mother and I were never that close. She called herself a 'Free Spirit' and that's why she ran away with my dad when she was only sixteen. They left Alaska and traveled around to all the oilfields. My mother loved being on the road, but when it came time for me to be born, my folks took me to California, and they stayed with my grandparents... from time to time. They still traveled a lot, so I didn't see my mom much, and of course my dad's parents knew nothing about my mom's family. I got a few letters from my grandmother, Adina, but she said nothing about being Amish or..."

Jürgen looked up from his soup. "Jewish?"

"Yes, I knew nothing about that."

Jürgen finished the last of his soup and stood up. "Okay, young lady, we'll talk after dinner, and you can ask me anything you like."

THAT EVENING, after Abigail helped with the dishes, Jürgen ushered her into the front room. It was the middle of November, and the fire in the enormous stone fireplace cast a wonderful light and warmth throughout the room.

Jürgen sat down in a large recliner chair and pointed to the couch. Abigail sat while Jürgen dug out a beautiful carved meerschaum pipe. "Mind if I smoke?"

"It's your house, Mr. Hirschberg, and anyway it doesn't bother me."

Jürgen tamped some tobacco into the pipe, lit it, and puffed a few clouds of smoke. The smell was nice and homey, and to her surprise, Abigail liked it.

"So, young lady, what's troubling you?"

She looked at the old man in surprise. "What makes you think I'm troubled?"

"Told ya I learned to read people when I was a kid. You're

unhappy about what I said... either about you being Amish or being Jewish."

Abigail took a deep breath. "I know nothing about the Amish, so that's not it. It's about being Jewish."

"What bothers you about that?"

"Well, you see, Tommy, I mean... well, Tommy told me that the Jews, especially the ones who live in Israel, are terrible people. He says they stole their land from the Palestinians and they've been occupying land that's not theirs since 1948. He says they are an apartheid state and treat the Palestinians badly. He says the Palestinians are an oppressed people and won't be free until the Jews give them back their land."

Jürgen shook his head. "Ah, Mr. Tommy rears his head. Well, young lady, I can tell you this. Mr. Tommy is about as ignorant as they come. Spouting a line that a bunch of Jew-haters made up, a story that's absolutely untrue."

"But he studied it in college."

"Yeah, he probably read it in something that George Lincoln Rockwell or Henry Ford wrote or maybe someone from one of those liberal churches who think that God is done with Israel and the church has taken Israel's place. Do you know anything about the actual history of Israel and the Jews?"

"Well, no, only what Tommy said."

"See, girl, that's one problem with people these days. They don't do their own homework. They don't actually look into the important questions and do their own research." He reached down and pulled a book from the row of books under the end table. "First, did you know that there has never been a nation called Palestine with an actual government run by Palestinians? Let me read you this excerpt from Mark Twain's book, 'Innocents Abroad.' He wrote it in 1867." Jürgen opened the book to the page with a marker in it. "This is what he observed about 'Palestine' while riding through the Jezreel Valley on horseback." He read...

"There is not a solitary village throughout its whole extent—not

for 30 miles in either direction. There are two or three small clusters of Bedouin tents, but not a single permanent habitation. One may ride 10 miles hereabouts and not see 10 human beings."

He continues. *"Of all the lands there are for dismal scenery, I think Palestine must be the prince... Can the curse of the Deity beautify a land? Palestine sits in sackcloth and ashes. Over it broods the spell of a curse that has withered its fields and fettered its energies."*

Jürgen closed the book. "Palestine was the name given to the land of Israel by the Romans in 136 AD after the Jews, who had been living there for two thousand years, revolted against Roman rule—the Bar Kokba revolt. The Romans put it down brutally. Historians estimate they killed hundreds of thousands of Jews and enslaved or exiled thousands of others. They completely depopulated the region of Judea. Then they plowed salt into the land and renamed the ancient nation of Israel Palestina, which was a corruption of the name Philistia. The Philistines were Israel's greatest enemy, and the Romans could think of no greater insult to the Jews than renaming their country after the nation that had plagued them throughout their history."

Abigail knit her brow. "How do you know all this?"

"My mama's father was a professor of history in Germany and a Jew. The Nazis sent him to a concentration camp, but my *daed* rescued him and brought him home from Europe in 1945. He lived with us until he died. I sat at his feet to study. He taught me everything I know."

"But Tommy said Israel stole the land in 1948..."

"What Mr. Tommy told you was either ignorance gone to seed or a deliberate attempt to turn you against the real owners of that land. It's called anti-Semitism, and it's still going strong. You see, the Jews were scattered throughout the world for two thousand years after the revolt, but they always knew they would come home one day."

"How did they know that?"

"It's all in the Bible."

"But isn't that just a collection of stories that try to get people to behave the right way? What about the Palestinian people? Tommy says they are the most oppressed people group on earth."

Jürgen stood up. "What does that little boy know about oppression? He lived in his mama's basement, got a free ride his whole life, never worked a day and got everything he needed. Wait here; I'll be back." He walked out of the room. In a minute he came back. He was holding a black binder. "My sister Adina was an excellent writer. She wrote this when she was seventeen. It's the story of how my mother and father, Gerd and Emily Hirschberg, met and how they came to America. Would you like to hear it? You might learn something about real oppression."

"Yes, I would like to, Mr. Hirschberg."

Jürgen sat down and opened the binder. "Make yourself comfy, this will take a while." He began to read.

"The Amish Menorah..."

THE AMISH MENORAH

DUST AND THUNDER – 1936

"*B*rrrr, Gunnar!" The huge *Suddeutsches Kaltblut* stopped in his tracks and looked around at Gerd. The horse pawed and snorted, eager to get on with the plowing. "*Beruhigen Sie sich, Gunnar! Seien Sie ruhig.*" As the horse quieted, Gerd took the traces off his shoulders and listened.

There! Thunder!

He looked up at the sky, but the calm blue heaven smiled back at him in perfect stillness.

Then again! A low rumbling in the distance, this time accompanied by the slightest shaking of the ground.

"*Aufenthalt hier, Gunnar.*" Gerd left Gunnar standing in the uncompleted row and walked to the top of the knoll that rose in the center of his fields. His eyes followed the line of the road winding off to the East toward Ixheim, then lifted to the low ridge beyond. He frowned. An immense cloud of dust drifted above the ridge. It seemed to move toward him. Gerd took off his hat and wiped his brow. The spring sun was scorching on his back, and sweat stained his shirt, but the soil beneath his feet was damp and held in place by the unplowed winter vetch.

There should not be any dust storms this time of the year, and not until the harvested fields are dry at the end of summer.

From below, Gunnar nickered, calling his master back to the field.

"Bleiben Sie Dort, Gunnar," Gerd called down to the horse. He looked again. Now the dust had come almost to the outskirts of the village, and he could see something emerging from the cloud. Gerd widened his eyes, and his hand lifted to shade them and get a better look. But he was not mistaken.

Tanks! Armored tanks. What are they doing here?

And then, out of the cloud, row upon row of marching, uniformed men with rifles over their shoulders and packs on their backs followed the tanks. As they drew closer, Gerd could see small armored half-tracks and *Kübelwagens* driving between the regiments. As he stood in bewilderment, he saw his neighbor Ernst Troyer coming down the road on the run on the back of a saddle-less horse. The young man galloped off the road and through the field, paying no attention to Gerd's plowed rows. He jerked the horse to a stop and catapulted off its back in front of Gerd.

"Gerd, Gerd ..." For a moment the lad could not catch his breath.

Gerd grabbed the boy by the shoulders. "What is it Ernst, what's happening?"

"The Germans, the army, Gerd ..."

"Ernst! Calm down. What about the army?"

"They've come, Gerd, they've come back to the Rhineland. I was outside the village when they marched by. They were cheering and waving and shouting about saving Germany's pride. I came to get you. The Elders want you to come."

"But the army cannot come here. The Allies demilitarized the Rhineland. No one can bring an army in here. It is against the treaty."

Ernst shook his head. "I am afraid Herr Hitler does not believe in treaties."

GERD HIRSCHBERG STOOD in front of the fountain that faced St.-Martins-Platz. Beside him stood Christian Guth, the elder of the Amish community in Ixheim, and Otto Schertz and Georg Nafziger, the two preachers. Around and behind them, the villagers of Ixheim gathered, an indistinct murmur of anxious voices filling the air. Uniformed German soldiers jammed the plaza. Armored vehicles blocked the entrances into the square except for one road, and Gerd watched as a large black German touring car with Nazi flags on the front fenders entered the town and motored toward them. The driver pulled to a stop in front of them, got out, raced around to the passenger side, and opened the rear door. A short, fat man got out. He looked almost clownish in his grey topcoat, which hung to the ground—and the tight collar of his black uniform blouse made his fat neck bulge, which squeezed his eyes into a pig-like stare.

The fat little man looked around at the simple farmers with obvious disdain. He saw the four men standing in front of the villagers and strutted up to them.

"Why are you not cheering and celebrating? This is a historic day for Germany. Our great Führer has put Germany into its rightful place among the nations of the world once again."

Christian Guth reached out his hand to shake the German officer's, but the man ignored the hand and looked at him with the same piggish expression.

"I am sorry, Herr ... Herr ...?"

"*SS-Oberführer* Heinrich Glauss. I am now in charge of this entire district. You are the mayor?"

"No, Herr Glauss—"

"Oberführer, *bitte!*

"Yes, Oberführer. No, I am not the mayor. This is a village of Amish farmers, and I am the elder of the village."

"Amish? Amish? You are the cowards who refuse to fight for our country?"

"We believe in the teachings of Jesus in the Bible, when he says that if your enemy smites you, turn the other cheek."

The fat little man looked hard at Christian and then stepped forward and slapped him hard across the face.

"And I say you are cowards."

Gerd started forward, but he felt Otto's hand hard on his arm. The movement did not miss the Nazi's notice. He turned. "So, this strapping fellow is not so ready to turn the other cheek, eh?"

He stepped up to Gerd, put his hands on his hips and stared up at the young farmer. "Why do you not wear the uniform of the Wehrmacht? You are sound and strong; you would make a good soldier."

Gerd remained silent. Otto spoke. "Please excuse my young friend, your honor. He is impetuous, but he loves his country. We are not at war, Your Honor, and there is no conscription."

"I am not talking to you; be quiet. I am talking to this fellow." Glauss turned back to Gerd. "If there were a war, would you fight? You seemed ready a moment ago."

Gerd swallowed. He could see danger in the German's eyes. "I apologize, Your Honor. It's just that Herr Guth is like a father to me and I ... I—"

"You did not wish to see him insulted, no? Well, the day is coming when you might wish you had the same feelings for the Fatherland as you do for this man. I ask again, would you fight?"

Gerd shook his head. "No, your honor, I would not."

Glauss stared at Gerd for a long time. Then he smiled. The smile was not friendly. "We shall see, my young friend, we shall see." The German officer took a few steps and faced the villagers. He lifted his arm in a victorious straight-arm salute and shouted. "Today is a great day for Germany. We have come back to the

Rhineland, the heart of our country. Our great Führer has ordered the reoccupation of this region to show the world that we are not toadies and lickspittles who lesser men or lesser countries can push around. We are Aryans, the purest race on earth. The world will soon find out they should not have humiliated Germany. Germany should have dictated the terms of the Treaty of Versailles, but the traitorous Jews and Communists betrayed us. Chancellor Hitler has cancelled all the reparation payments to the so-called allies, and now, we stand as the one nation that can light a beacon for the rest of the world to follow. Today is a great day; I wish you all to celebrate. Give praise to our victorious German army and our great Führer. *Seig Heil!*"

There was a moment of shocked silence. Glauss reached down, pulled his pistol from its holster, and fired a shot into the air.

"Give praise, I said!"

The people jumped in surprise, and a few toward the back of the crowd raised a weak cheer.

"*Seig, Heil!*"

The *Oberführer's* arm snapped up, and he screamed along. "*Seig, Heil!*" All the soldiers in the square followed, roaring their approval. The arms of the non-Amish villagers lifted into the Nazi salute, and they shouted along with the soldiers. "*Seig, Heil! Seig, Heil! Seig, Heil!*"

The Amish men stared at each other in horror. In a moment, the Germans had transformed their peaceful village into a Nazi rally. Glauss marched up to Christian and placed the pistol against his head. He glared at the others. "You Amish people will give praise to Germany or your elder will die."

The Amish looked at Christian, who stared straight ahead. Otto stepped forward and nodded to the villagers, who hesitantly lifted their arms and chanted along. Gerd was the last to raise his hand. Glauss smiled, waited for a moment, and then holstered his pistol. He turned toward the car, but before he left, he took Gerd by the arm and said again, "You will fight, my young friend, I promise you." Then he swaggered back to the car, where the driver was waiting to open the door. He climbed into the back seat, but before he did, he turned to Gerd once more and mouthed the words, "You will fight." He laughed as he signaled the driver to leave.

The door slammed, and the car departed in a cloud of dust, Glauss laughing in the back seat. The chants of "*Seig Heil*" slowly faded, and the citizens of Ixheim stood looking at each other in shame.

GERD SAT on the rough bench in Christian Guth's barn with the two preachers. Christian was reading from the Bible.

Aber ich sage euch: Liebt eure Feinde, segne tauft euch, tut Gutes denen, die euch hassen, und betet für die, die euch trotzig gebrauchen, und verfolgt euch.

Guth closed the book, then looked up and smiled at Gerd. "You were ready to fight for me, my son?"

Gerd nodded. "The man had no right to strike you."

"*Ja*, maybe he did not. But as I read, the words of our Lord remind us always to pray for those who use us evilly. Besides the fact that the Bible and our *Ordnung* teach us the ways of peace, it would have been very dangerous for you to assault the Oberführer. You would be dead now, and we cannot have that because you mean too much to Ixheim. You are the future of this congregation. I have been the elder here for a long time. Any days I have left are a gift from *du leiber Gott*."

Gerd shrugged. "But I am a simple farmer, and I am too young. I am not made to lead."

Otto turned to him. "The people of the village look up to you. You have great wisdom already. You will be the next elder. So, let us say no more about it. *Das ist ein Streit um des Kaiser's Bart.*"

Gerd smiled despite himself. "*Sie müssen einen Vogel haben.*"

The three older men looked at Gerd and began laughing. Gerd shook his head as he thought about the events of the day.

Perhaps the Nazi was right. Maybe I will fight if it is against such fools as him.

GEFÄHRLICHE TAGE

*G*erd sat in the kitchen thinking over the troubling day. An oil lantern burned on the stand by the door, and shadows flickered on the walls, dancing a strange, silent *Zweifacher*. His mother poured him a cup of coffee and set it on the table.

"We have fresh cream, Gerd."

Gerd nodded as she set the pitcher next to his coffee.

"What will happen, Gerd? What will Hitler do next?"

"I do not know, *Mütti*. From what I hear, he is a very determined man—determined to erase the shame of Germany's loss to the French and their allies in the war. He wants to make Germany into a great country again, but I do not know how that will affect us."

"I wish your father were here, Gerd. He would know what to do."

"*Ja, Mütti*, he would know."

There was a knock at the door that startled them.

"Who would come at this hour?" his mother asked.

Shrugging, Gerd stood and went to the door. Christian Guth

stood there. The old man looked haggard and worn, and his appearance surprised Gerd.

"What is it, Brother Guth?"

"May I come in, Gerd?"

"Yes, yes. Please forgive my rudeness."

Gerd ushered the old man into the kitchen. His mother bustled up another cup, but Christian shook his head.

"I had a visit from the head of the Gestapo after you left."

"The Gestapo? What is that?"

"The Gestapo is Herr Hitler's *Geheimstaatspolizei,* his secret state police. They have taken over Zweibrücken—moved into the Mayor's office, and they have moved troops to the border and closed it."

"Closed it? But how will our people from Lorraine be able to attend church?"

"They will need a special pass, and they will have to cross at a checkpoint near Saarbrücken. But that is not all." The elder looked down.

"What Christian? What else?"

"Hitler's Nazis have been using racial biologists since 1933 to examine the Mennonites and every other people group in Germany for racial purity. The consensus was uniform," Christian said. "Mennonites, according to these scientists, were more Aryan than the average German."

Gerd nodded. "That's not surprising. Swiss Mennonites began coming to Zweibrücken in the 1600s. And since then, they have emigrated all over Germany."

"And France," said Christian.

"What does that have to do with us?"

"The Gestapo chief, a Major Steinmann, said that because of our racial purity, the Mennonites and the Amish are crucial to the German war effort."

"War effort! But we are not at war, Christian."

"Steinmann must have trusted me, for he used that phrase

and intimated the reoccupation of the Rhineland is just the first step in Hitler's plans for Germany."

"But how will we serve the war effort ... if a war comes?"

"Steinmann told me that the Anabaptists, the Amish and the Mennonites, are the most competent of all German farmers, and they are very obedient to the law. He thinks, given our racial purity, obedience, and loyalty, they could use us to lead other German farmers in a great agrarian revolution, so that the coming *Reich* would have more than enough food to supply the population if difficult times came."

"But ... but, Christian, does he understand we will not lead an effort to support great violence?"

"Yes, Gerd, I explained that to him, but he is certain that when the time comes, we will understand our duty."

"What are we to do, Christian?"

Christian stood and shook his head. "I have been the elder of this congregation since 1907. I shepherded it through the Great War, and we faced persecution for our anti-violence stance then. Now will be no different. We will just have to obey Christ, no matter what." He shrugged.

"But, Christian, these men are different; I could see it in that fat *Oberführer* Glauss's eyes. These men are evil, evil to the core. We will despair the day they came goose-stepping into our quiet village. Only bad will come of this, and turning the other cheek will not change that. I do not think our people can bear what is coming."

"It is not only our people I fear for, Gerd. There are those among us whom these men do not consider racially pure enough to be part of this great new German kingdom."

"Who are they, Christian?"

"Well, and again only because he considered me his equal as a German, he named them: Gypsies, homosexuals, the retarded, communists, the unproductive ... but their greatest target is the Jews."

"The Jews? But the Jews have been in our country for centuries. They have assimilated. How many of Germany's brilliant musicians, doctors, teachers, or businessmen are Jews? There are Jews in every village and city. Tov Weiss in Zweibrücken helped my father with a loan to get us by in a poor year. Our family considers him a friend."

"We are isolated here in Ixheim, Gerd. We have not seen what the Nazis are doing. They have used propaganda campaigns to promote hatred of the Jews. They convinced the public that it was Jews and communists who sold Germany out, and that is why we lost the war. Now, Hitler is using them as scapegoats, blaming them for Germany's economic and social problems. Most Germans believed him, and that is one reason the Nazis rose to power."

"But why did he tell you all this?"

"It was a tip-off and a warning, I think. The Nazis are hunting Jews, particularly those Jews who are communists, and sending them to camps. They are confiscating Jewish property and issuing anti-Jewish decrees, which have eliminated the rights of Jews."

"But Christian, this is terrible. Why did we not know of this?"

"We are in the world, Gerd, but not of it. Ixheim is far from the centers of power. And there was one last thing."

"What?"

"Again, I think he was sharing as one Aryan to another, but there was a threat there, too. They will consider anyone who befriends a Jew or helps them a traitor to Germany, and that person will suffer the same fate as the Jew they help."

The two men looked at each other with dawning horror.

THE GOLDEN EDGE of the sun was just flashing over the far hills, and brilliant rays reached up, turning the indigo of night into the rose of dawn. Gerd walked out into the frosty March morning. Christian's words had kept him from sleep the whole night.

What are we coming to? Gefährliche Tage I think, dangerous days.

The bite of a fading winter gnawed at him as Gerd picked up his hoe and began to dig the early spring weeds out of his mother's garden plot. As the sun crept higher in the sky, he warmed to his task, and soon, he stripped off his shirt. He stood there in the sunlight, tall and bronzed, his muscles rippling like ropes as he attacked the wet dirt, partly in anger but mostly in disgust at what he had heard the night before. Streams of sweat ran down his back and shoulders—soon his skin was steaming in the brisk air.

"Working hard again, Gerd?"

The voice startled him, and he pivoted to find Hilda Knepp standing at the corner of the house, a basket under her arm. He could not mistake the unbridled interest in the young woman's eyes, as she looked him over like she would a young horse.

"I brought some *eier* from our chickens for your *mütter*. I hope I am not disturbing you." Hilda edged a little closer. "You seemed deep in thought. Is something troubling you?"

Gerd had known Hilda all his life. Over the years, they had fallen into an unspoken understanding that one day Gerd would court her. But as Gerd grew older, he saw things with an eye tempered by the realities of life. He was not sure Hilda was right for him, if only in temperament. Gerd was a serious young man, with the responsibility on his young shoulders for managing the large farm his father had left him when he died in a logging accident. Hilda was mischievous, outspoken, and even brazen in her attention to Gerd. When they were younger, she had driven many an innocent Amish girl away from Gerd's attention. Gerd had puffed up to think a girl as pretty and buxom as Hilda was so interested in him, but as he grew older and wiser, Hilda's possessiveness wore on him.

THEN OTHER HANDS applied pressure on Gerd to court Hilda. Hilda's father was poor in land, and the thought of his daughter being brought into the family of the man who owned the largest farm in the area prompted him to speak to Gerd's mother about a marriage. But Magda knew her son would make his own decision in his own time. She just shook her head at Jakob Knepp's importuning.

"Gerd will come courting when he's ready, Jakob. He has much responsibility, and I think he has not yet made time for other things in his life—things like a wife and *kînder*. He will come around soon; give him time."

"But Mother Hirschberg, Hilda is not getting any younger. It is time for her to go out from under my roof and into the house ... and bed ... of her own husband." He shrugged and smiled a deprecating smile. "Don't you want *enkelkinder*? I do."

Gerd's mother shook her head. "In the Lord's time, Jakob, in His time."

Unable to enlist Magda Hirschberg's help, Jakob had sent Hilda by the Hirschberg place every day on the smallest of pretexts, a transparent ploy that was becoming more obvious to Gerd each time Hilda came.

"Gerd?"

Gerd shook his head and smiled at the girl. "Oh, *entschuldigen Sie*, Hilda. My mind wandered. The coming of the Army has changed many things in Ixheim already, and I fear for the future of our community. There are bad days ahead, I am thinking."

Hilda flushed and then stepped closer. "*Ja*, Gerd, I think you are right. Even I can see that." She put down the basket of eggs and twisted her hands. "That is why I must speak my mind. I know you will think me *aufdringlich*, too forward, but I thought we understood that when you accepted baptism into the church, you would ask my father for permission to court me. Well, you are almost twenty years old, and your baptism is soon. I am already nineteen, and as you say, the coming of the Germans brings great uncertainty. Don't you think it is time for us...? I mean, well, time for you...?" She trailed off.

"... to come courting?" He looked at the girl who stood before him. Hilda was beautiful in her own way—curvaceous, with flaxen hair and cornflower eyes—a picture of the idealized German woman.

If I could tame your tongue and your jealousy ...

"Can you not speak? Before I shame myself?"

Gerd nodded. "You are right, Hilda, you are right. Give me a few days, and then I will come see your father."

Hilda's face lit up, and she took two quick steps toward Gerd, but he held up his hands. "We shouldn't even be alone together like this. Go home now. I will see you in a few days."

She nodded, then threw her apron up over her burning face, turned and ran down the path to the road.

Gerd shook his head.

I don't know, Gott. I suppose this is the right thing to do, but you must show me if I am right.

EMILY

*I*t was dusk, and Gerd was walking his fields as he always did when he needed to think something through. To the East, the twinkling lights of Ixheim sparkled like fireflies among the rills and swales that marked the sloping hills of the Saar Valley. Below him spread the Amish farms of Ixheim. From his knoll, he could see the lantern light coming on in the windows of the Oesch farm, and on the farm just below, Hans Gingerich led his team of black Friesians toward his ancient barn.

Gerd chuckled.

Hans's blacks are a good team, but my Gunnar can out-pull both of them together. Ja!

His steps turned toward his own barn for his nightly check of all his animals. The old door creaked open at his push, and he stepped into the dark mustiness of the rambling structure. His great-great-great-grandfather Hirschberg had built the barn when Gerd's ancestors first came from Switzerland almost two hundred years before to settle in the *Rheinland-Pfalz*. Huge hand-adzed beams held up the walls and the loft, and many stalls and storage rooms stretched back into the darkness. He took the lantern from the shelf by the door, struck a match and lit the wick. The soft light spread into the gloom where he could see his cows chewing their cuds in their pen. Back to the left, he saw Zwingli the goat's horns peeking up over the boards of her stall, and he heard the tiny bleats of the new kids as they nursed.

When he came to Gunnar's stall, the magnificent horse was standing still with his ears up. Instead of nuzzling up to Gerd looking for the apple Gerd kept in his pocket, he snorted and stamped.

"What is it, Gunnar?"

Gerd looked around, then reached up to stroke the animal's neck, but Gunnar pulled his head up and stared into the darkness at the back of the barn.

Gerd heard a small sound, like the rustle of mice in the corn bin. "Mice again, Gunnar, *Ja*? I thought my traps had rid us of those pests." Gerd turned and walked to the corn bin. He waited, then jerked open the lid, hoping to catch the little *störenfriede* at work, but the bin was clear, full to the brim with last fall's harvest and not one dropping to mark the presence of field mice.

Hmmmm, what was that noise?

Then Gerd heard it again—a movement in the hay, back in the dark.

Cat, maybe...

"Hansli? Hansli, are you hunting for dinner?" But no answering yowl came from his mother's big tomcat.

He walked toward the back of the barn, lifting the lantern, and looking in each stall. Nothing. He was about to turn back when he heard another sound, like the whimper of a small, trapped animal about to meet the hunter. Gerd walked around the last stall and lifted the lantern again. There—a movement in the hay mound, something dark, almost hidden by the pale straw. Gerd stepped forward, holding the lamp high.

"I see you in there; come out."

There was a sigh of resignation, the hay stirred and a face looked up at him. Long dark hair with bits of straw stuck in it, large luminous green eyes, pale lips, a slender neck rising out of a dark sweater.

A girl!

The girl stood. She drew her shoulders back. Gerd could see she was trying not to be afraid. Her chin lifted, her eyes blazed up as though a fire had been lit behind them. Her thick black sweater clung to her trim form, rolling down over her hips and hiding the top of her black skirt, which reached down to the tops of her walking shoes. She was lovely.

"Come out of there."

The girl stepped into the light, her movements graceful ...

Like a dancer!

"Who are you? What are you doing in my barn?"

"I am Emily. I am hiding."

"Emily who? And who are you hiding from?"

"Emily Weissbach. I am hiding from the Gestapo."

"But why?"

"I am a Jew."

Gerd stared at the girl for a long moment. Christian's words from the night before came back to him, and he felt a strange rush of ... fear ... premonition?

At last he spoke, almost to himself. "A Jew! But I am forbidden to associate with Jews."

A wince passed over the girl's face, and she shrugged. "I know you are. That is why I am hiding."

"Where did you come from?"

"Munich. I am trying to get to France."

"You cannot get out of Germany. The border is closed. You need a pass."

"I was hoping to sneak across."

"Impossible. The Germans have already strung barbed wire,

and they have started patrolling the border day and night. They do not want the French army to come in and throw them out of the Rhineland, so they are extra vigilant. No one can get through."

For the first time, the girl's face lost its bravado, and she stared at Gerd with those enormous eyes, as though beseeching him for something. Without a sound, she sank back down into the straw and put her hands over her face. She was quiet for a moment before her muffled words came out from behind her hands, a whisper, a sob.

"What am I to do?"

Gerd stared down at her. Then he crouched down beside her. "Where is your family? Father ... mother?"

Her face hardened for a moment, then tears came. She reached up and wiped them away with an abrupt movement of her hand. "They are in Dachau camp. My father is a communist, and they rounded him up. They took my mother with him. They killed my brother."

"But that is terrible. You are alone?"

"Yes, I have no one to help me." She reached under the straw and pulled out a cloth suitcase. "I have only these few things. Three days ago, I was coming home from the store, and I saw all the cars in front of our house. The soldiers dragged my father out. His face was bloody, and he had no coat. They threw him into the back of the car. After that, they dragged my mother out and put her with him. My brother came running out and tried to get my father out of the car ..."

"What?"

She brushed more tears away. "The office in charge shot him in the head. They left him lying dead in the street. I could hear my mother screaming as they drove away."

"*Mein Gott!*"

"I waited until it got dark and went in the back door, got some things and some money and took the bus to Saarbrücken."

Gerd shook his head in disbelief. *"Kumm."* He helped the girl up and led her to a bench along the wall. She sank down on it, her face pale.

"Have you eaten anything, Emily?"

"Not for a day. We were partway to Saarbrücken when several army trucks and soldiers on motorcycles passed the bus. I heard one passenger say the Nazis were sweeping the countryside looking for collaborators, enemies of the Reich. The man said there would be roadblocks and checkpoints, so when we stopped to use the restrooms in Landstuhl, I slipped away and I've been walking ever since, hiding in the woods and keeping out of sight."

"But that's thirty kilometers, and you walked it? Come into the house and eat."

Emily's face went white. "No, I must not. You are already in danger for seeing me. Anyone else who does so is also in danger. Just let me hide in the barn for a while and rest."

"I'll go get some food from the kitchen then. Stay here. I'll be back soon."

The girl started up from the bench, her face ashen-hued. Gerd put his hand on her shoulder and smiled. "Do not be afraid. You are safe here, I promise." He went to a shelf and pulled down a thick woolen blanket. "Wrap yourself in this. It still gets cold at night in these parts."

Emily took the blanket with a grateful glance.

"Stay here. I will return."

GERD WENT INTO THE HOUSE. Magda was in the living room, sewing a quilt. She looked up as he passed. "There is hot soup on the stove and fresh bread on the table. Sit and eat."

Gerd shook his head. "I will take something out to the barn. One kid is very thin, and I want to make sure it is nursing. I will eat there."

Magda shook her head and smiled. "Maybe Jakob Knepp was right. Maybe you need a family so you could take care of your *kinder* the way you take care of those goats."

Gerd went on into the kitchen and poured hot soup into a tin. He cut some slices of bread and cheese and grabbed an apple from the barrel. "Don't wait up, *Mütti*, I may be late coming to bed."

"All right, son, all right."

Gerd went out the back door and made his way to the barn. The girl jumped up when the door opened, but she sank back down when she saw it was Gerd. He brought her the food and placed it beside her. She looked up, the blanket wrapped around her, her hair disheveled, her face drawn, but to Gerd, she was beautiful.

"There is a barrel of fresh water by the door and a basin if you wish to freshen up first."

She smiled a shy smile and went to the barrel. Her movements were sure and smooth, and she carried herself with poise. "Don't look, please," she said. "I need to take my sweater off." Gerd turned away. He heard the rustle of her sweater slipping off and the splash of the water as she filled the basin. Gerd could hear her slosh the water on her face with a gasp. He smiled.

"I forgot to warn you; it is cold."

"Cold? It is like a Greenland glacier."

She washed for a few more minutes, and then Gerd heard the rustle of the sweater sliding back on. "I'm decent now."

Gerd turned. Emily was standing in the lantern's light, the straw brushed from her hair and her face brighter, more alive. She twisted her long black hair up in a bun behind her head, and the powerful lines of her face were now very prominent. Her deep green eyes were almost otherworldly—her nose was straight and her jawline firm. She smiled, and her teeth were straight and white. He stared at her.

"What?"

He turned away, embarrassed; he was blushing. "Come, Emily. Eat the soup while it is hot. You must get your strength back."

She sat down on the bench and ate. She ate as she had done everything else, with poise and grace, no movement wasted.

Gerd got up his courage. "Excuse me, but may I ask you something?"

"Yes?"

"Are you a dancer?"

Emily looked at him with a curious smile on her face. "Yes, but how did you know?"

"Just the way you carry yourself. I saw a ballet dancer once, and you remind me ... I snuck away to watch a troupe when they came to Zweibrücken; I should not have done so."

"*Ja*, why not?"

"I am Amish. We try to keep ourselves apart from the world as much as possible. We follow the *Ordnung* and we—"

She looked at him and laughed. The sound was bells and fire-flies and a brook splashing down a mountain cliff.

"Why do you laugh?"

"Because you are telling me everything about yourself, but you have not even told me your name."

He felt the heat of another blush.

This is foolishness. I have never blushed in my life. I am ...

"Gerd. Gerd Hirschberg. That is who I am. This is my farm. I live here with my mother. But tell me about your dancing."

"It might be too worldly for you." She laughed again.

"No, please."

"I am nineteen. I began dancing ballet when I was five. When I was thirteen, Mary Wigman chose me to be her protégé. I danced in a company that featured *Ausdruckstanz*, Expression Dancing. I worked with choreographers like Rudolph von Laban and Mary, and our company was just beginning to gain international recognition when the Nazis came to power. They deemed our style of dance degenerate and disbanded our company. All dancing in Germany was now to be for the glory of the Nazis, but Mary would not go along. Rudolph, however, adhered to the Nazi ideals and became director of the national company. I traveled to America with Mary in 1933, but when we returned, it was to a different Germany. Mary still dances and choreographs under the Ministry of Propaganda, but she is not a Nazi." She picked up the bread. "Do you wish to know more?"

"I'm sorry, please finish your dinner."

She took bites of the bread and then went back to the soup with relish while Gerd sat without speaking. The girl eyed him while she ate. At last, she set the tin aside, wiped her mouth with a cloth and looked up. She started to say something but stopped.

"What is it?"

She drew a deep breath. "I need help. I need to get out of Germany. I have money, so I can pay you. If what money I have is not enough, I have something else of great value I will give you if you help me." She turned and reached into her bag. She pulled out a strange-looking object that was golden and gleamed in the lantern light. Emily handed the golden thing to Gerd. It looked like a candlestick but had eight branches with cups on the ends and a ninth in the center.

"What is it?" Gerd asked.

"It is a *menorat Hanukkah,* a menorah. It is pure gold. If you help me, I will give it to you. My great-grandfather, who was a renowned goldsmith in Poland, made it."

Gerd stared down at the golden menorah. The light from the lantern reflected off the many facets of the beautiful craftsmanship. It seemed almost alive in his hands.

Come to the light, Gerd; I am here. I am the light.

Gerd looked up, startled. "What did you say?"

Emily shook her head. "I said nothing."

Gerd shook his head. The warnings about Jews thundered in his head, but as he sat with this beautiful girl, he did not care. He handed the menorah back to Emily.

"I ... I will help you ... but I do not want your money."

Is this you, Gott? Is this you?

A REFUGE

*a*fter their conversation, Gerd made a bed for Emily in the hay and went into the house. His mother was in her room, and Gerd heard her praying as he passed the door. That night, phantoms filled his dreams—men in tight-fitting black leather jackets with no faces chased him through the fields waving guns, shouting at him.

"Where is she? Where is she?"

He woke before dawn, his sheets soaked in sweat and his stomach churning. He swung his legs over the side of the bed and sat with his head in his hands. The girl flustered him. She was a Jew, an enemy of the German nation—or so they said. He should report her. But she was also lovely, intelligent, and she needed help, his help.

I don't believe in accidents, Gott. You must have something in mind. Of all the farms in the Saar Valley, she chose my barn to hide in. She could have picked Hans's barn or Ernst's, but she is here, in my barn.

Gerd sighed, stood up and found his clothes in the semi-darkness. On most mornings like this, the first rays of the sun peeking over the eastern hills delighted him, and he loved the light fragrance of forsythia flavoring the day like a small spoon of sugar in a cup of black coffee, the eager greeting of his animals as he laid the hay and grain in their feeders. But today he was in a dark mood.

If I am caught harboring her, it will mean the camps for my mütter and me. I should give her some food and a map and send her on her way. Her being here can only mean trouble.

He remembered her eyes as she crawled in between the blankets he laid out for her—he had seen gratitude and hope in them before they closed and she was asleep. He stood for a very long time staring down at her face. In repose, she was exquisite—her face was a carved marble mask, symmetrical, perfect—but she was alive, and her soft breath stirred a piece of straw beside her mouth. At last, he knew if he stayed, he would stay all night, just looking at her, drinking her in. He blew out the lamp and turned toward the door. As he laid his hand on the latch, a small voice came out of the darkness and stirred a fire in him he had never known.

"Good night, Gerd. Thank you."

Now he walked back and forth in front of the barn, thinking. He looked up at the sky. "What should I do, *Gott*?" he cried.

"Do about what?"

Gerd jerked around. Hilda Knepp stood there, looking at him. She had a shawl over her shoulders and a basket in her hand.

"Hilda! What are you doing here?"

She stepped back, with a quizzical look on her face. "I come every day with something for your *Mütter*. Papa slaughtered hogs yesterday, and I have brought some hocks for her to make *Schweinshaxe* with. What's wrong with that?"

Gerd shook his head. "Nothing, nothing, except I thought we agreed you should stay home for now, until... until I come to speak to your father. We do not want to start gossip among the villagers."

Hilda laughed. Next to Emily's laugh, hers sounded coarse and brazen, like a mule braying in a barn. "They are already gossiping, Gerd. They are wondering when you will visit our house in your courting clothes." She smirked.

"*Ja, Ja*, Hilda, I will come, but until then I think it is best that you stay home."

"What were you asking *Gott* about?"

"Uh... oh, that. It's personal."

"Don't you think we should share our personal things now? I mean, after all..."

"When we marry, Hilda, you will learn everything about me. I warn you though, you may not like what you find out."

Hilda shook her head. "What's wrong with you today? You are not like yourself."

Gerd was silent for a moment, staring at Hilda. The buxom blonde girl, who had once seemed attractive, now looked blowzy and cheap.

"Look, Hilda. The coming of the Nazis changed everything. Christian has told me that when he passes, the village will make me the elder. I do not think I am ready for that. It troubles me, the responsibility."

"But all you need is a good wife by your side, a wife to help you and ... give you children." She smirked again, and Gerd felt sick inside. *And lord it over the other women in the village because you are the wife of the elder and the mistress of the largest farm in Ixheim.*

"Hilda, give me the basket. I will give it to *Mütter*. Thank you and thank your father for us. I ask you to return home. I will come to see your father soon."

Hilda frowned and handed over the basket. "When you come to see him, please bring the old Gerd." She turned and walked away with her nose in the air.

Gerd went into the house with the basket, his emotions in turmoil. His mother was preparing breakfast for him—some *Schwarzwaelderschinken*, some sliced Gouda cheese, and a large cup of coffee. She was slicing a large piece of pumpernickel bread. He hesitated as he sat down at the table.

"*Mütti,* I need to tell you something."

"What, Gerd?"

He looked up and hesitated.

"What is it, Gerd?"

"Someone is hiding in the barn."

She turned. "What! In our barn?"

"Yes, *Mütti.*"

His mother went back to the bread. "Well, tell them to leave. People can't just come and stay in our barn."

"I can't make her leave."

This time his mother turned clear around and looked. "Her?"

"It is a young girl, and she is a Jew."

Gerd's mother put down the knife she was using and moved to the table. "A Jew! But Gerd, you told me the Nazis forbade us to associate with Jews. She puts us in danger; she must leave."

Gerd shook his head. "There is more to it, *Mütti.* She needs help. The Nazis will send her to Dachau if they find her. They will kill her ... or worse."

Magda looked hard at her son. Then she noticed something in his face. "Gerd?"

"I cannot send her away, *Mütti,* I must help her."

Magda sat down beside her son. "Gerd, what is it?" She took Gerd's face in her hands. He looked away, but she drew him back and stared into his eyes. "Look at me, son."

He struggled, but her hands were insistent, so he surrendered. "*Mütti ...*"

Magda gasped. "Gerd! What has happened to you?"

"I don't know, *Mütti,* I don't know."

"But you only met her last night."

"Yes, but... but... Oh, I don't know what happened. She is beautiful and intelligent and, I... I..."

Magda took Gerd by the hand. "Take me to see her."

"But, *Mütti,* I promised ..."

"Nonsense. I live here too. If we are to save this young woman, we cannot have secrets." She pulled him to his feet. "*Kumm.*"

Together, they went out to the barn. When Gerd entered, Emily was just coming to the door, her suitcase in her hand. "Gerd, I ..." Then she saw Magda and stepped back. Gerd saw the fear on her face.

"I am sorry, but my mother—"

Magda stepped past Gerd and over to Emily. "Do not be afraid, my child. I am Magda, Gerd's mother. I made him bring me. We will help you, but you must withhold nothing from me."

"Help me?"

Magda chuckled. "My son hides nothing from me. He never has, and he never will. When I looked into his eyes, I knew he would help you, no matter what the cost. So, I will help too. What is your name? Where are you from?"

The girl hesitated and answered in a quiet voice. "Emily. Emily Weissbach." She looked at Gerd and then at Magda. "I am from Munich. My father is a lawyer, but he was involved with the Communist Party, and the Nazis came for him. They took him and my mother away and killed my brother."

Magda looked at Emily, then stretched out her arms. Emily hesitated and then stepped into the circle of love, tears streaming down her face. She sobbed as Magda held her.

"There, there, *mein kleines Mädchen,* it will be all right. You are safe here."

Gerd stood, shifting from one foot to the other, at once embarrassed and yet grateful to his mother. The sobs subsided. Magda reached into her pocket and pulled out a clean linen handkerchief. Emily wiped her eyes and blew her nose. She looked at Gerd.

"I will leave. I have put you in danger, and I do not want any harm to come to you ... or your mother." She glanced at Magda.

Gerd shook his head. "You cannot leave now; it is too dangerous. You should stay here for a week, two perhaps. The French will not come—they are afraid of the Germans. If they weren't, they would be here already. Soon, the Germans will know this and will not be so vigilant. Then we can get you into France."

"But you can't hide me from your neighbors for two weeks."

Magda smiled and took the girl by the arm. "Yes, we can, but if anyone asks, you are my cousin Freda's daughter, Emily, and you are here to visit us for a fortnight. You are from Weisbaden, not Munich, and here to visit your Amish kin. Your family is Mennonite, so Gerd will tell you about us—who we are and what we believe. Gerd is right. The Germans will relax their guard in a few weeks, and we will get you across the border. Until then, you will stay with us."

Emily looked at Gerd. "But... but..."

Magda took her by the arm. "It is settled. Now come and eat breakfast."

A LIGHT FOR THE DARKNESS

*E*mily sat at the table and ate quietly. When she finished, she looked up at Gerd. "Are you sure this is what you want to do?"

Gerd nodded. "I think Gott has brought you to us for protection. Beyond that, I only know our faith tells us to strengthen the weak hands and the knees that are feeble, and make straight paths for your feet, so the limb which is lame may not be put out of joint, but be healed."

Emily looked surprised. "You know the *Mikra?*"

"What is the Mikra?"

Emily smiled. "It is the Jewish holy book. It contains the *Torah*, which are the teachings of Moses, the *Nevi'im*, the books of the Prophets, and the *Ketuvim*, the writings, what you call the Psalms and the Proverbs."

"I do not know Mikra," said Gerd. "That verse is in the New Testament of the Bible, in the Book of Hebrews."

"Book of Hebrews? I have read a little of your Bible, but not this Hebrews. That verse is in Isaiah the prophet's writings. He says, 'Strengthen ye the weak hands, and confirm the feeble knees. Say to them *that are* of a fearful heart, be strong, fear not:

behold, your God will come *with a* vengeance, *even* God *with* a recompense; he will come and save you.'"

Magda laughed. "I can see you two will have much to talk over. But first, we must do something about you. You cannot say you are Mennonite if you do not look Mennonite. I have some old clothes that will fit you. I wore them when I was a young girl. In those days, I was as shapely as you are, Emily, but the years have added some padding here and there."

To his surprise, Gerd blushed again.

"*Kumm,* Emily. Let us be about your transformation."

An hour later, Emily was a Mennonite girl. Magda had given her some things and sent her into the guest bedroom to change. When she emerged, she was no longer the modern-looking girl of the night before. In place of the dark sweater, skirt, and hiking shoes was a long, pale-blue skirt buttoned up at the side, a plain dark-blue blouse with long sleeves, and a dark scarf.

Gerd noticed that the clothing did nothing to hide her beauty. *You could dress her in a pair of overalls and she would still be lovely.*

"I found no zippers anywhere, Magda," she said as she adjusted her skirt.

Magda laughed. "And you will not. Although we abandoned hooks and eyes long ago, the non-Amish still call us *Häftler.* You will find only buttons." She handed Emily a pair of wool shoes. "And these will keep your feet warm, but they are not for outdoors. I have some rubber boots for that. Now, go sit with Gerd. He will tell you of our ways."

GERD AND EMILY sat at the kitchen table together. Gerd started. "My family came to Ixheim in 1648 from Switzerland. Back then, we were Mennonites. My great-great-great-grandfather built this house and the barn where I found you. We have farmed here ever since. We were Mennonites when we came, but now we are Amish. We are still Anabaptists in that we do not believe in infant baptism, but we follow Jakob Amman, not Menno Simons. We have set ourselves apart from the world, and we have a very strict set of guidelines we follow to keep us on the right path. We call them the *Ordnung,* and we have passed them down from generation to generation."

Emily nodded. "Much like the Law of Moses in the Torah. Are your laws written in a book?"

"No, but our elders have been very careful to keep the *Ordnung* pure, because it provides our community's foundation."

"What are some of these rules?" Emily asked.

"Well, Amish men do not wear beards until they are married, marriage can only take place between baptized members of the church, we do not use modern conveniences such as automobiles or gasoline engines, we do not get involved in politics, and we cannot divorce our spouses. But the most important thing is we do not take part in any form of violence."

Emily nodded. "What happens if you violate these laws?"

"If the offender will not repent of their sin, we excommunicate them—what we call *Meidung* or shunning. Then they are in the *Bann.*"

"What happens to them?"

"We keep them separate from the community. We may not eat with them or ride with them or accept gifts from them. They cannot attend church. The community will still give them help if they need it, and we can converse with them, but until they repent, they cannot be a part of community life."

Emily frowned. "This sounds very harsh."

Gerd laughed. "That is what the Mennonites say, and that is why we are no longer part of the same church." He paused. "But these are simple rules, and no one will question you on the articles of your faith. Now tell me about you."

Emily's eyes flashed. "What do you want to know?"

"Well, for one, I want to know about that candlestick. It's beautiful."

"It's not a candlestick; it's a lamp stand. The menorah uses oil instead of candles. This is a *menorat Hanukkah,* a Hanukkah menorah."

"Hanukkah?"

Emily laughed at Gerd's struggle with the word. "Hebrew can sound harsh, Gerd. Many of the words sound like the speaker has a bone caught in his throat. It's spelled with an 'h' but you pronounce it as though it has a 'ch' in the beginning."

"What is ... Chanukah?"

Emily laughed again. "That's closer. Hanukkah is the Festival of Rededication. It celebrates the cleansing of the Temple in Jerusalem after its defilement by the Syrian Greeks under Antiochus Epiphanes. It's also called the Festival of Lights. The menorah is the lamp stand God commanded Moses to put into the Tabernacle, which later became the Temple. Most menorahs only have seven branches, but you see this one has nine. That is to commemorate a great miracle associated with Hanukkah."

"Miracle?"

"I would have to tell you the entire story, Gerd."

Gerd looked at the girl. In that moment, he realized he wanted to know everything about her—her childhood, her family, her religion, if she belonged to anyone...

I don't want her to belong to anyone; I want her to belong to ...

"Gerd?"

"Please tell me the story, Emily."

She cocked her head with a quizzical look on her face, a gesture that Gerd would come to know well.

"Please."

Emily sighed and nodded. She rose from the table and went into her room. She returned in a moment with the menorah and set it on the table between them. A stray beam of sunlight filtered through the window curtains and fell upon the lamp. The gold surface reflected the beam in a flash of light.

I am the light of this world!

"What?"

"I said nothing, Gerd."

She cocked her head again, and he realized she captivated him—the way she moved, the beauty of her face, the light in her eyes.

"Shall I go on?"

Gerd nodded.

Emily picked up the lamp and revolved it slowly in her hand. "Ever since the days of the Babylonian captivity, one country after another has conquered Israel. In 329, Alexander the Great conquered the Jews. After he died, his generals divided his empire into four parts, and Israel became a pawn between the Egyptians and the Syrians. In 167 BC, the Jews of Judea rose in revolt against the Syrians, who were the current overlords. The Syrians tried to eradicate the Jews and all their customs, including keeping the temple holy. They vandalized it and even sacrificed a pig on the great altar in the Holy of Holies. This enraged the Jews, and under Judah Maccabee, the Jews conquered the city. They set about to cleanse the temple, a process that took eight days. But they had only enough consecrated oil for one day. As the story goes, the menorah kept burning for all eight days. They say it was a miracle of God."

"Do you believe the story, Emily?"

"Well, I am not so sure, but I know enough of my people believed to make the eight days into a festival of its own, even though Moses did not include it in the Torah. And they created the *menorat Hanukkah* with its nine branches to commemorate the eight-day miracle."

Gerd took the lamp and stared at it. "But what is the ninth cup for?"

"It is the servant cup. You light it first, then light each of the others from it. Each night another cup is lit until all of them are burning on the eighth night."

"So, this Feast of Dedication—it is in December?"

"Yes, we have observed the Feast of Dedication for thousands of years, celebrating God's protection and the victory he gives his faithful people who continue to worship him in the face of persecution."

"Such a time as this, perhaps?"

Emily's face paled. "Yes, such a time as this."

"In our Bible, there is a mention of the Feast of Dedication—in the Gospel of John, the tenth chapter." Gerd rose and fetched his Bible off the bookshelf. Thumbing through the pages, he came to John and turned to the tenth chapter. "Ah, here it is. 'Then came the Festival of Dedication at Jerusalem. It was winter, and Jesus was in the temple courts walking in Solomon's Colonnade.' This is the chapter where Jesus claims to be one with the Father."

Emily's eyes widened. "Such a claim is blasphemy to the Jew. The Torah is very clear. 'Hear, O Israel: The Lord our God, the Lord *is* one!' This Jesus cannot also be God."

Emily's face was lit with an inner fire as she spoke. Gerd could not take his eyes away. Finally, he spoke. "May I ask a question?"

"Yes."

"You said your father was a communist, yet you know so much about the Torah and your faith. How is this?"

"My father decided that to be German, he must put away his Jewishness. He wanted to become 'assimilated.' During the Weimar Republic, he associated with Walter Sholem, intrigued by the communist theories Sholem was putting forth. The Nazis arrested Sholem as soon as they came to power, but my father had not been high in the party, so they did not come after him right away. If he had not continued speaking out against the Nazis ..." She paused and looked away for a moment. When she turned back, there were glints of tears in her eyes. "My mother tried to go along with Papa in his beliefs, but in her heart she was an observant Jew. So, despite my father's objections, she taught me about my faith."

"She taught you about Hanukkah?"

"Yes, and we celebrated every year. For my father, the occasion was more cultural, but the celebration held deep meaning for my mother. She used to say, 'The miracle of Hanukkah shows Israel is the light of the world.' My mother firmly believed the nation of Israel will be born again, which will be proof to the world that the Jews are God's chosen people." Emily picked up the menorah and stood up. Her face was haggard. "I am tired, Gerd. I did not sleep well last night. I think I will lie down for a while."

Gerd nodded. He watched as Emily walked away.

I am the light of the world. Jesus said that of himself. Perhaps the Jews and the Amish are much closer than we know.

HEARTS ENTWINED

*N*ow the days passed in a blur. To Gerd, it was as if Emily had always been there. Her smile, her voice, the lithe and lovely movements of her body, the way she cocked her head when she was thinking—all this filled Gerd's waking thoughts and swept through his dreams. He went about his work, but it was no longer the routine of drudgery he once faced each morning; instead, in every task he saw meaning and purpose. Gerd became more in tune with the cycle of the land and watched with newfound joy as his crops burst forth from the ground. His thoughts became focused on the Creator of the universe at work all around him, and they quickened him with a new understanding of his place in the great warp and weft of the days flowing around him like a river.

And instead of finishing his work in the quiet moments of a simple meal with his *mütter* and then the quick fall into an exhausted sleep, he came home from the fields to a house filled with laughter and the aroma of dishes Magda had not cooked in years filling the house, as his mother showed Emily how to prepare them. The two women would giggle like schoolgirls sharing secrets, and Gerd wondered if they were talking about him. After supper, Gerd would sit up with Emily and they would converse into the small hours, but when he awoke in the morning, he was refreshed and ready for the day.

Life flowed back into the house, a life that was born and radiated forth from the Jewish girl's innermost being and filled Gerd's days with unimaginable joy and his nights with peaceful repose. The world outside seemed far away, the Nazis and soldiers in the towns and villages were merely unwelcome visitors and his world —the simple ways, the fields, the growing crops, the land itself pulsing with life—became centered in the girl in his home, hidden away and safe.

Though they did not dare go far from the house, Gerd and Emily began walking to the knoll and sitting together as the crisp March evenings passed into the star-filled nights of early April. Often, they spoke together, but tonight, they were silent, sharing the moment, yet trembling on the brink of some great turning in their lives. At last, as a dove called a melodious note to warn its mate to return to the nest, Gerd turned to the girl beside him.

"Emily ..."

She turned, and her face reflected the growing rose of the clouds above. The luminous green eyes opened wide, set like emeralds in her alabaster face. There was a question in those eyes and on her lips. "What is it, Gerd?"

But he could see she knew what his words would be, for he saw the answer in those wonderful eyes. His powerful arms lifted, and she was in them, as close to him as she could come. She turned her face to him, the question gone, replaced by a beseeching and a touching of their souls through their eyes. His lips found hers, and they were embracing—the fire and smoke that once flowed from newborn mountains at the creator's command enveloped and consumed them.

Hours later they came back to the house, awed by the stillness of the night and the enormity of the road they had stepped onto. She brushed his fingertips with hers and went up to her room. Gerd went into the kitchen. Magda was there, shelling some early peas from the garden. She looked up and smiled. "When will you marry Emily?"

Gerd stopped in surprise, taken aback by her words. He laughed and shook his head. "How well you know me."

"This means you will leave the church. Have you considered that?"

"What if Emily becomes Amish?"

"She is a Jew, Gerd. She loves her faith. She will not convert. You can help her understand her Messiah has already come. But no, she will not convert. You will go to the elders and tell them you will marry this Jewish girl, and Christian will weep, for you are taking his dream away. You will go to Hilda and tell her, and she will hate you with a burning hatred. We may have to leave our farm and find a new life far away. And that is the path you have chosen. But I will walk it with you as long as I am able."

Gerd was silent at his mother's words. The wisdom in them weighed down on him like boulders pressing upon his chest, but the weight was not enough to make him cry out. He knew the hands of this Jewish girl held his life and his future, and he would not turn his back on what *der leiber Gott* had given to him. "Yes, *Mütti,* that is the path I have chosen."

"No, Gerd, you cannot."

The soft voice surprised him, and he turned. Emily was in the doorway, tears on her face. "I cannot let you give up everything in your life for me—your farm, your faith, your community, your future. I will leave tomorrow, and I will find my way to France."

Gerd stepped toward her, but she raised her hands and moved a half-step back. "No, Gerd, please…"

Gerd pushed past the upraised hands and took her in his arms. She was trembling like a leaf in a storm, and tears ran down her face. "No, Gerd, no ..." Her arms came around him, and she was weeping and holding him with a strength that would have crushed a lesser man.

He caressed her hair and kissed her on the cheek. "You will not leave me, Emily. *Gott* has sent you to me. We will find a way through the darkness."

———————

"YOU WHAT?" said Christian Guth.

"I have met the girl I want to marry."

"Hilda?"

"No, Christian, not Hilda."

Christian Guth rose from the chair he was sitting in. "What do you mean? Is she Amish? Where did you meet her?"

"I found her in my barn. She was hiding from the Gestapo. She is a Jew."

Christian's face paled, and he sank back down. "A Jew," he whispered. "A Jew?" he said again as though he had never spoken such a word.

"Yes, Christian, she is a Jew."

"But... but... you cannot marry a Jew. You know what the Gestapo said. Anyone who aids or harbors a Jew will suffer the same fate as they do. It could bring destruction down on our entire community. And what of the *Ordnung*? It forbids you to marry someone not of our faith." He began wringing his hands. "Gerd, you will go under the *Bann* if you do this."

"I have considered that."

"You would throw away everything you have—your faith, your community, your position as elder?"

"I will have her, and she is enough."

"But if the Nazis find out ..."

"How will they find out? Will one of us betray me? She will live under my roof as my wife, and things will go on as they are until it is safe to get across the border. If people ask, I will tell them she is the daughter of my mother's cousin. Then, when we can leave, we will go to France."

"Your farm, Gerd. What of your farm?"

"I will sell it to Hans. He has often hinted that he would buy it if I ever tired of farming. It would make him the largest land-holder in the Saar Valley."

"Your mother?"

"She knows and will go with us. She loves Emily as I do."

"How long has this Jew been with you?" He spat out the word.

"Since the day after the Germans came."

"Three weeks? You have known her for three weeks, and you want to marry her? I am not hearing this," said Christian. "This is insanity."

"That may be, but it is what I will do."

Christian tried a different tack. "Ever since your father died, I have been like a father to you. I am asking you not to do this. I have decided you will take my place when I die. Everyone expects it. I expect it."

Gerd shook his head. "You are like a father to me, Christian, and I will always love you for that. But I never agreed to your plan for my life. *Gott* has sent this girl to me, and I will not go against his will."

Christian rose from his chair, his face flushed. He shouted at Gerd. "His will! His will! How would an ignorant, stupid boy like you know God's will? I am the elder, and I will tell you what God's will is! You must send this woman away, forget you ever met her and let things go back to the way they were. You will marry Hilda, and you will become the next elder."

Gerd looked at Christian as he ranted. When he finished, Gerd stood up. "I cannot put her away. Our love has already gone too far to do that."

"What? You... you... you have been intimate with her?"

"Yes, Christian, I have been intimate with her. That is why we must marry as soon as possible."

"So, you add sexual sin to your litany of transgressions? You will repent now and forget this madness, or you will go under the *Meidung*."

"I will not repent."

"But what about your vows?"

"You forget, Christian. I am not yet baptized into the church, and I have not taken those vows. My life goes a different way."

"Well, since I have not baptized you, I cannot place you under the *Bann*. But you will be as a stranger to us. You will have no relationship with the Amish of the village. We will not do business with you, and you will not be part of our community activities."

"But you do business with the other non-Amish. Why will you treat me so?"

"To teach you a lesson. You know the *Ordnung*, and you are violating it."

"That is too bad, Christian. I hoped you would help me with this."

Christian stood and went to the window. "Violation of our laws separates you from Gott, with no hope of redemption."

The law does not save you, Gerd.

"What?"

Christian turned. "I said ..."

"Not what you said, Christian, but what *Gott* said."

"And now you are a prophet?"

"The *Ordnung* does not save you, Christian. Only Jesus can do that."

"What!"

"The righteous shall live by faith. It's in the Old Testament and the New. There is no difference between the Amish and the Jews who try to keep the Law of Moses. We all need a Messiah, Christian."

Christian began trembling, and he choked out his words. "This Jew has bewitched you, Gerd. You have lost your mind. Get out of my house!"

Gerd felt a great sadness rise in him—sadness because he was leaving the things of his boyhood behind, because he was giving up his home and community, and because he had lost the friendship of someone he thought would always love him.

If any man will come after me, let him deny himself, and take up his cross, and follow me.

Gerd stood at the door and looked back one more time at the old man, who stood with his back turned.

I will follow you, Lord, though I do not know the way.

Then he stepped through the door and out into the world.

NEW LIFE

"*Y*ou wish to marry?" The gray-haired man smiled up at Gerd and Emily from behind his cluttered desk. He had a kind face.

"Yes, Pastor Jügens." Gerd looked at Emily, and she smiled and nodded.

"Well, Gerd, I am surprised you come to me. Won't you marry in the Amish church?"

"I have decided not to continue in the Amish faith."

A look of concern crossed the pastor's face. "I have known your family all my life, Gerd. Your father and grandfather were friends of mine. I cannot imagine a Hirschberg who is not Amish in Ixheim."

"Yes, Pastor, but that is what I have chosen."

"Does it have anything to do with ..." he looked over at the girl.

"Emily, Pastor. My name is Emily, and yes, the problem is me. I am not Amish."

"Oh, I see now, Gerd. Emily is not Amish, and Elder Guth refuses to marry you?"

"Yes, Pastor, that is the heart of it. I have come to you because you have always been a good friend to our family, and I know I can trust you."

"Trust me with what?"

"Emily is Jewish."

The words crashed like heavy stones onto a metal floor. The pastor looked down, took off his glasses and passed his hand over his eyes. Then he looked back up. "You were right to come to me." He got up and went to the door and checked and then paused at the window and looked out. "The Nazi regime has not assimilated all the Protestant churches. Since you have trusted me, I will trust you. I am a member of the Confessing Church. Deitrich Bonhoeffer is one of our leaders. We decry the populism, the *Deutchland über alles* heresy that has overtaken the German church. Anti-Semitism is everywhere in Germany now and contradicts what the apostle Paul says about the Jews." Pastor Jügens sat down at his desk. "I will help you, Gerd. Though you put us in great danger. If the Nazis find the girl, they will take her to the camps, and you will go too." He shrugged, "And me."

Emily spoke up. "How do we get around the Nuremberg laws forbidding mixed marriage?"

The pastor smiled. "Actually, I think God has given you a window of opportunity. The Germans are preparing for the Olympics—scheduled for Berlin this summer. Foreign reporters and observers have flooded the country. Hitler is trying to make it look like Germany is peaceful and everything is perfect—a German utopia. He has ordered his officials to relax the discriminatory laws and remove all anti-Semitic signage and newspapers from public places. If we go today, we can get the license. I have a good friend at the city office—he will not be so particular with his questions."

"Won't we need birth certificates?" Gerd asked.

"Yes, do you have them?"

"Mine is at home, but Emily ..."

"I brought mine when I left Munich," Emily said. "I thought I might need it when I got to France. I have my passport too, from when my dance troupe went to America."

Pastor Jügens nodded. "Excellent, excellent. We should have no problems. Get your birth certificates and meet me at the *Standesamt*. You must marry before the official, and then we can have a private ceremony in my church ..." he paused and looked at Emily. "If it is all right with you."

Emily paled.

"What is it, Emily?"

"Nothing. It's just I always hoped my father and mother would be at my wedding, and I would watch my husband smash the glass at the end of the ceremony."

Gerd moved to Emily's side. "What is this smash the glass?"

Emily wiped a tear from her eye. "In a Jewish wedding at the end of the ceremony, we wrap a glass in a cloth, and the husband steps on it. It symbolizes the Roman destruction of the Temple in 60 AD. It is a reminder that even amid joy, we recall the pain and losses suffered by the Jewish people. And there is more. Marriage is a covenant. In Judaism, we make a covenant by cutting or breaking something. At Sinai, the tablets were broken—at the wedding, broken glass cuts the covenant."

Pastor Jügens nodded. "I have been to Jewish weddings, and I always wondered." He stood and put his arms around Gerd and Emily. "*Kumm, meine Kinder,* we have things to do."

———

THREE DAYS LATER, Gerd Hirschberg and Emily Weisbach stood in the small chapel of Pastor Jügens's church and repeated their vows. Magda stood beaming beside the pastor's wife. At the end of the ceremony, Gerd took Emily in his arms and held her as though he would never let go. "*Du bist ein Geschenk Gottes,* a gift from *Gott,* and his goodness amazes me."

Emily kissed him on the cheek. "And you have saved me. I

was lost, and you found me. Thank you, Gerd. I will always love you." She kissed him and held him, and in that moment, he knew a great love that burned him with ferocious heat but did not destroy him.

Like Moses at the burning bush ...

He nodded to his mother, who handed him something wrapped in a cloth. Gerd put it on the floor, raised his heel and smashed the glass hidden in the folds of the cloth. Emily gasped and cried.

"What is it, my love?" Gerd asked.

"You, Gerd. You are so kind. This makes the day perfect— well, almost perfect."

"What is missing, Emily?"

"Just this," Emily said, and she stood on her tiptoes to whisper in his ear.

"What?"

Emily blushed and nodded. Gerd felt tears start in his eyes. He said nothing, but his heart was bursting with the blessings of this day.

———

HILDA KNEPP STOOD outside the church in a drizzling rain. Through the window, she could see the happy couple embracing, and the few guests gathering around to offer congratulations.

This Jew witch thinks she can come into my world and steal the man I was to marry? But she does not know me. I will not go without a fight. She will regret the day she ever set eyes on Gerd Hirschberg.

Hilda turned and walked away into the gray drizzle.

———

THAT EVENING, Gerd and Emily walked together, their hands entwined and their shoulders touching. The rain had stopped, and the world seemed fresh and alive with sounds and fragrances Gerd had never noticed before. They passed a brilliant yellow bush, and the light fragrance lifted to Gerd's nose like a passing thought. Emily smiled. "The forsythia only smells that way after a rain. They were my mother's favorite plant."

The green low hills of the Saar basin rolled away on all sides. Gerd's gaze took in the Hirschberg farm—the house, set in a sheltered swale, the barn behind it, the knoll that had become their special place.

"Gerd?"

"Yes, my love?"

"Can't we stay here? I love this land."

Gerd looked around him—this farm was all he had ever known. As a young boy, he had followed his father from place to place, learning every aspect of the work—the plowing of the fields, the care of the animals, harvesting the crops. And as he pictured his childhood, the thought came to him he had never really loved the work, but work was the way he garnered his father's approval and recognition. When he failed at something, his father was harsh in his quick condemnation, so Gerd had learned to focus, to concentrate on his tasks and in that way to draw forth his father's meager approval ...

Like poison from a wound ...

He shook his head. "I don't think it will be possible. When I looked in the *Oberführer's* eyes the day the German army came to Ixheim, I saw evil. The Jews have already had their rights taken away, and although Hitler has relaxed his anti-Jewish ranting for the moment, I do not think this time of grace will last. But we still cannot cross into France, for we have my *mütter* to consider, and it has only been six weeks since the Germans came. They are strutting along the border, daring the French army to push them out of *das Rhineland*. But I do not think the French will come. We will wait until the Germans are less vigilant and then we will go."

"But this is your home, Gerd."

"My home is where you are, Emily." He paused and turned to her. "I must confess to you I have only been a farmer because my father and grandfather and their fathers before them farmed this land. I only stayed here, stayed Amish, because I wanted to please my *Daed*. And when he died, I had to provide for my mother. But I have other dreams."

A look of surprise crossed Emily's face. "Other dreams?"

Gerd paused, and suddenly he was shy. He had never shared his heart with anyone in this way, not even his *mütter*. He took a deep breath. "Yes, I want to raise and breed horses. That is all I have ever wanted to do, but my father rejected the idea as too worldly. He told me I had to concentrate on farming because I was a farmer and Amish, and that was all I ever would or could be. I raised Gunnar from a tiny colt. His mother died when he was born. He has been my only horse. But many times, I have wished I could breed him and populate this land with strong, beautiful horses."

Emily took Gerd's hand and laughed. The sound was a delight to Gerd. "It may take many years to discover everything about you, Gerd Hirschberg." Her face grew thoughtful. "When I was in America with the dance troupe, we traveled to Colorado. Oh, Gerd, you cannot imagine the beauty of the mountains there. It is as though the heavens and earth touch each other everywhere you look. And in the west of America, there are horses, beautiful horses. When we were going on the train, I saw men on horseback driving vast herds of cattle—the horses were small, but so agile, and the men riding them are called cowboys. It was as though adventure stories had come to life. Perhaps we can go to America and go to the West. It is a big land, and it is a place where dreams can take root and grow."

Gerd took his wife in his arms. "Yes, Emily. Let us leave this place of war and beating drums and marching armies and go into the West. We will find a new life, and we will build our dreams, you and me and... and..."

"Our baby?"

"Yes, beloved, our baby." They turned back toward the house, and as they did, the gray clouds opened and a dazzling sunset spread before their eyes. The moisture in the air reflected the light in a beautiful prism of color.

"Look, husband. God's promise is there before us. We will go into the West."

Gerd's heart beat fast, and his body was alive as it had never been before.

Yes, my love. We will go into the west ...

I AM THE LIGHT

$\mathcal{I}$ Am The Light

The next morning, Gerd told Magda the news of her coming grandchild. Magda went off humming an old German lullaby with a broad smile on her face. Emily came into the kitchen and sat down with Gerd. "Your *mütter* is happy, *Ja*? She is not ashamed of me?"

Gerd reached over and caressed the alabaster skin of her face. "She is your mother now too, and she loves you almost as much as I do. She knew from the first day I told her about you, I had fallen in love with you. The night," Gerd blushed ... "That night, when we came home from the hill, she asked me when I would marry you. She somehow knew we were already one in our hearts. No, she is not ashamed."

"And I love her too ..." Emily hesitated, then put her hand on Gerd's arm. "Do you think she would mind if I put my menorah on the kitchen shelf? It is the only thing I have to remind me of my home."

"Please bring it out. We will give it a place of honor."

Emily went into her room and came out with the menorah.

Gerd placed it on the top shelf between his mother's good china pieces. The morning sun coming in through the window caught the facets of the beautiful menorah and lit the walls with golden diamonds. Emily sat next to Gerd as he sipped his morning coffee. As he gazed at the lamp stand, he closed his Bible and looked at Emily. "Tell me more about the celebration that this candle..." he paused, "I mean, lamp stand, represents."

Emily smiled. "The feast is Hanukkah, the festival of lights, and we pattern it after the Feast of Tabernacles. Tabernacles is one of the seven feasts of the Lord given to Israel to mark the important events of the year. The feasts start at Passover, which marks the day the Lord sent the destroyer angel over Egypt and killed all the firstborn in the land as a warning to Pharaoh."

Gerd nodded. "Yes, I've read about that. The Israelites marked their doors with the blood of a lamb, and the destroyer passed over."

"Yes, that is right. There are five more feasts—Unleavened Bread, where devout Jews only eat the same bread the Jews ate when they came out of Egypt, The Feast of First Fruits when the people of Israel brought their first harvest to the priests at the temple and waved it before the Lord, and the Feast of Harvest, which celebrated the summer harvest. I think Christians call it Pentecost."

Fifty days after I rose from the dead ...

"Fifty days after First Fruits?"

Emily cocked her head. "Yes, how did you know that?"

Gerd shrugged. "I must have read it somewhere..."

Emily went on. "After that come the three most important feasts in September or the Jewish month of *Tishri*. First is the Feast of Trumpets, what we call *Rosh Hashana*. It marks the first day of the Jewish New Year, and the rabbis blow the shofar. Beginning on *Rosh Hashana*, there is a ten-day period known as the *Yamim Nora-im*, Days of Awe. Nine days after the first day we observe *Yom Kippur*, the Day of Atonement. That is the day where

Jews ask for forgiveness of sins committed during the year. When the temple still existed, this was the day that the High Priest entered the Holiest Place and brought the blood of a sacrifice and asked God to forgive all the sins of Israel."

Without the shedding of blood, there is no remission of sins.

"That reminds me of a scripture from the Book of Hebrews."

Emily smiled at Gerd. "You mention the Book of Hebrews often. I think I must read it."

"What about the Feast of Tabernacles?"

"The Feast of Tabernacles often goes by another name, 'The Season of Our Joy.' The feast reminds us that God is the Great Shepherd who dwelt among his people, to protect and bless them wherever they wandered. Every Jew looks for the day when God will come back to his people and save them, as he did in the days of Moses. We chant the *Hallel*, the psalm of praise, during the celebration in the synagogue and wave palm branches."

"Palm branches?"

Emily nodded. "Yes."

Like Palm Sunday, when Christ rode into Jerusalem ...

"How do those psalms go?"

Emily thought for a moment. "Well, I don't have them all memorized, but the ones I like are 'Save now, I beseech thee, O Lord: O Lord, I beseech thee, send now prosperity. Blessed be he that cometh in the name of the Lord: we have blessed you out of the house of the Lord.'"

For I say unto you, ye shall not see me henceforth, till ye shall say, blessed is he that cometh in the name of the Lord ...

This intrigued Gerd. "I know that Scripture, but it is in the book of Matthew. So why is Hanukkah patterned after this feast?"

"During the time of the Maccabee revolt, Antiochus defiled the temple, and no Jew could go into it to celebrate Tabernacles in September. Two months later, when they recaptured Jerusalem, the Jews celebrated Tabernacles in December. They spent eight days cleansing the Temple and then celebrated *Sukkot* by waving palm branches and chanting the Hallel. Ever since then, Jews celebrate Hanukkah and the Feast of Tabernacles in much the same way. The *menorat Hanukkah* is lit in the homes of observant Jews to commemorate the miracle of the lights when the Maccabees restored this important feast."

Gerd sat for a moment. "I think we have much in common, wife, though our worlds are so far apart."

Emily blushed and lowered her eyes. "Wife," she whispered.

Gerd took her hand and bowed his head. When he lifted it, he could feel tears on his face. "I am thanking God for you, today and every day, my Emily. You have given me much to think about. For the first time in my life, I feel that *Gott* himself is speaking to me—through you."

A WEEK AFTER THE WEDDING, Gerd went to Hans Gingerich. Hans saw him coming through the field between their farms and motioned him into the house. He looked nervous. "Gerd, it is good to see you. I ... I ..."

"You don't want any of the village to see me here, right?"

Hans shrugged. "Christian has forbidden all of us to speak to you, but you have been my best friend since we played in my father's apple orchard, so I welcome you. Sit down. I will get us some coffee."

Hans brought coffee and sat across from Gerd. "Do you remember sitting here waiting for a piece of my mother's *Stöllen?*"

Gerd smiled at the memory. "You know what has happened, Hans?"

"You will marry the Jewish girl? Christian told us."

"We married a week ago." Gerd saw the look of dismay on Hans's face. "Do not worry, Hans, we are leaving in a few days. That is why I have come. I want to sell you my farm."

"Your farm? But Gerd, there have been Hirschbergs on that farm since the 1500s."

"Yes, and now there will not be a Hirschberg there." He shrugged. "Things change, Hans. *Gott* has sent me a wife, and he is moving me out of the rut I have lived in all my days. He is opening something new and wonderful in me. Every day I am with Emily, I discover how little I know about him. I feel like nothing in my life has been real until now." He looked at Hans. "Do you want the farm? I give you a fair price."

Hans nodded. "I will buy the farm. Gunnar too?"

Gerd hesitated. Gunnar? Gunnar was the best horse in the Saar Valley, but there was no way to get him to America. "Yes, Gunnar too, Hans."

Hans shook his head. "Now I know you are going away, or you would not sell Gunnar. Where do you go?"

"We will go to America."

"America? But this is so far. How will you get there?"

"I do not know yet. I must get to France first. Once we are there, we will be safe and can figure everything else out."

"What will you do without land?"

"I will go into the west of America, find some land, some splendid horses, and raise them."

"Horses! *Ja,* Gerd, you have always loved them." Hans reached across the table and took Gerd's hand. "I will miss you."

"Ah, but Hans, now you will have the biggest farm in the entire valley, and your dream will come true. You will have a second house where your sons and grandsons can live."

Hans laughed out loud. "If I ever find a wife, that is." He shook his head. "No one knows me like you, Gerd."

Gerd stood. "I am only taking a few things. I am leaving the furniture so you can do with it as you wish. All the tools are in the barn—you know where they are. I must go now."

"I will bring the money tomorrow, Gerd."

"*Ja, Gut.* Tomorrow then." Gerd rose and turned to go.

"Gerd?"

"You must be careful."

"Careful? *Ja*, the Soldiers..."

"Not of the soldiers, Gerd, but of the Amish." Gerd turned back in surprise.

"The Amish?"

"*Ja*, Gerd. The Nazis think the Amish and the Mennonites are the purest Aryans of all the Germans..."

"Because we come from Switzerland, *Ja?*"

"*Ja*. They have held a few meetings where they have been shouting about the superiority of the German nation, how we are the highest race of men, and the Mennonites are at the top. Many of the pompous asses in the village have swallowed the bait, hook and line. Now, they go about with swelled heads, looking down their noses at anyone who is lesser than themselves. They have already driven the gypsies out of the valley."

"But the gypsies are the best people with horses. Who will shoe the farmer's teams?"

"They will have to figure that out, for the Gypsies are gone. The Nazis called them subhuman, so the Mennonites joined in driving the *Romani* out. Now they are looking for Jews."

"Do you think they would betray me? These are people I have known all my life."

Hans hesitated. "Hilda Knepp ..."

"What about Hilda?"

"I have seen her in the *Oberführer's* company."

"The fat one?"

Hans nodded.

Gerd laughed despite the tightening in his stomach. "I would expect no less of her. She will find a bed to sleep in where she can trade her body for a place of importance. But the *Oberführer*?" He laughed again.

"But she hates you now, Gerd, and she has made that plain. She has been planting seeds among the villagers who sympathize with the Nazis. I will come as early as I can. You must not wait a few days, for that will be too late, I think. You must be ready to go as soon as I bring the money. It is no longer safe for you in Ixheim."

No longer safe in Ixheim? How can this be?

"Thank you, Hans. I will be ready."

"What about my mother?"

Glauss pulled a handkerchief from his pocket and dabbed his nose. "You have proven me right. I said you would fight, and you did." He glanced at Magda. "I am not a cruel man. I have need of someone to cook and clean for me, and since your mother is not the one who married the Jew, I will show mercy by giving her a place in my house."

You mean by making her your slave!

Gerd looked at his mother. As Glauss turned away, he mouthed the words, "I will come back ..."

Magda nodded. The soldiers grabbed Gerd and Emily and shoved them out the door. As Gerd passed the *Oberführer's* car, he saw Hilda Knepp sitting in the back seat, a look of raw hatred on her face.

If I could reach you now, Hilda ...

GERD AND EMILY stood on the platform of the Saarbrücken train station with a group of haggard-looking people. Soldiers carrying guns surrounded them on all sides. A light rain had come through an hour before, and Emily shivered next to him. They had been there for hours and now at last, around midnight, a train with four or five boxcars was pulling in. Next to Gerd stood a tall, husky man in a ragged coat with an unkempt black beard. His hair was uncombed and wild, and he was missing some teeth. A strange odor arose from his clothes. Emily grimaced when he came and stood next to them. He smiled, but Gerd looked away.

He looks crazy.

The man smiled again. "I know I don't look so good. I looked better before the Nazis threw me in jail ... and smelled better, too. And I had all my teeth then."

Gerd looked back. The man, despite his wild appearance, had a kind face and piercing eyes. Gerd swallowed his distaste and reached out his hand. "I am Gerd Hirschberg. This is my wife, Emily."

"I am Joshua, Joshua Rosen."

Emily looked up. "You are Jewish?"

Joshua nodded. "*Ja.*" He looked around. "Most of these people are Jews also, and many of them are communists. *Herr* Hitler has little tolerance for either, I'm afraid."

Emily looked closer. "You are Joshua Rosen from Munich?"

"*Ja,* the very one."

"You know my father, Émile Weissbach?"

Joshua looked closer, and a broad grin creased his battered face. "Why, it's little Emily all grown up. Yes, I know Émile. We were comrades together on the front lines of the Revolution with Werner Sholem. I have been to your house in Munich often, but long ago, and you were much younger. Also, I have not been a Communist for many years."

Emily cocked her head. "You haven't? I thought you all swore to die for the revolution."

Joshua smiled. "Yes, but I found another way, a better way."

Gerd looked at the man. His face lit up, and what had been a marred landscape seemed to shine with an unearthly light. "Yes, I found ..."

There was a shouted command, and the doors on the boxcars up and down the line slid open with a crash. The soldiers shouted. "*Reinkommen. Beeil dich. Schnell nein.* Get in! Get in! Hurry!" The soldiers behind them herded them toward the boxcars. Many in the crowd cried out, but the soldiers kept shoving. When they got to the boxcar, Joshua jumped up into the open doorway, then turned around and gave his hand to Emily as Gerd boosted her up. When they finished loading everyone onto the cars, the soldiers slammed the doors shut. Bodies jammed together in the darkness, but Joshua wrapped his arms around Gerd and Emily and herded them to a corner where they slumped down with their backs to the wall. The train whistle blew several short blasts and moved, at first slowly, then faster as it pulled out of the station. They were on their way to Dachau.

THE TRAIN TRAVELED through the night. After a few hours, the faint light of dawn came through some cracks in the walls of the car. The train began slowing and blasting its whistle. Gerd rose and squinted through a crack. "We are coming into Stuttgart. I saw the sign. The train looks like it is pulling off onto a siding."

The train stopped with a jerk. There was a rattling at the door; it slid open, and a guard stuck his head in. He grimaced and leaned back. "You stink like animals," he shouted, "but what can you expect of Jews? *Raus mit dir. Machen Sie es schnell.* Everyone out! The commander gives you ten minutes to do your business."

The people in the cars clambered down, and the soldiers herded them off a few yards onto the dirt. "Go!" shouted one soldier.

Emily blushed. "Here? But they will all see."

Joshua took off his coat and made a shield, and Gerd stood on the other side. When Emily finished, they did the same. Then the soldiers herded them back onto the train. But they remained on the siding. Soon, Gerd could hear another train coming, going in the opposite direction.

"It is a troop train," he said. "It is full of soldiers probably headed for the German border."

They sat on the siding for many hours as more troops and equipment clattered by headed west. At one point, the guards opened the doors and handed in big milk pails full of water and some tin cups. The people in the boxcar shared the water and then handed the pails back out. Then the guards let them out to stretch their legs.

Gerd watched as the young soldiers laughed among themselves and made fun of the prisoners. "These soldiers seem friendlier than the ones I met in Ixheim."

"Look at them," said Joshua. "They are only boys. This is all a lark for them, a picnic. They are the vanguard of the great Germanic kingdom, and they are all puffed up with themselves."

"They do not fear a war?"

Joshua shrugged. "They do not understand. Most of them weren't even born when the Great War ended. They never saw the death and destruction, the millions killed. I was in the infantry. I saw the horrors of the Somme firsthand. Thousands of men being blown to bits, parts of bodies everywhere in the mud." He shook his head. "These children knew the hard times of the Weimar, but then Hitler came and everything got better. He is a god to them. He is restoring Germany to greatness. They are German and easily pushed into arrogance. They will all have a sad end, I am thinking."

Soon the sun went down, and darkness grew. As the last train went by, two trucks rolled up. Soldiers in black uniforms got out. A man in an overcoat with a death's head emblem on his cap walked up to the commander of the guards and spoke rapidly in German. The commander saluted and shouted orders to his men, who went to the trucks and got in.

"*Shutzstaffel,*" hissed Joshua, "SS. This is not good."

The man with the death's head shouted at his men, and the SS troops began pushing everyone back into the cars. The doors slammed shut, and the train rolled. Joshua was silent.

Emily whispered to Gerd. "I feel sick. It is probably the pregnancy. I will try not to throw up."

Joshua looked at them. "She is not feeling well?"

Gerd shook his head. "She is nauseous. I think it is the baby."

"You will have a baby?"

Emily smiled. "Yes, but not for a while."

Joshua looked at Gerd. "You are not Jewish?"

Gerd shook his head. "No, I am ... I was Amish."

Joshua smiled. "Now, that's something. A Jewish girl and an Amish Christian, both under the law, both going to Dachau, and their law cannot save them." He laughed uproariously.

Gerd frowned. "I don't see what is funny."

Joshua calmed down and put his hand on Gerd's shoulder. "I'm sorry, I did not mean to offend. It seemed funny at the moment."

Emily spoke up. "You said you are not a communist anymore. Are you a practicing Jew?"

Joshua hesitated. "Well, yes, and no."

"What does that mean?"

"I am still a Jew, and I am observant. I celebrate all the feasts and long to go to Jerusalem. But I have added something."

Just then the whistle blew, and the train jerked. As the train picked up speed, Emily shouted over the noise. "What have you added?"

Joshua grinned. "I have found my Messiah."

The train sped on through the darkness.

WHO HAS BELIEVED OUR REPORT?

*I*t was late in the night when a hoarse whisper followed by a hand shaking his shoulder awakened Gerd. "Gerd? Gerd?"

He had been dreaming of horses. He was astride a huge black stallion running like the wind down a gravel road, the horse's hooves pounding out a relentless rhythm. He awoke to the clacking of the train wheels on the track.

"Gerd?" It was Joshua. "I found something. I was sitting here, and something kept poking my backside. When I looked, I found water had rotted a section of the floorboards. I worked at it and got a sizeable chunk out. I think we can pull up enough of the floor to crawl out."

"Crawl out?"

"Yes. We must escape, and soon. I do not feel good about these SS troops. Something bad will happen, I think. You don't want your wife and baby to end their days in a Nazi concentration camp or worse, do you?"

"No."

"Then help me pull these boards up. We must do it while the

train is moving or the guards will hear." Joshua scooted over and showed Gerd the place where the floor was rotten. It looked like the floor had been getting wet for a long time. There was a hole where Joshua had broken some pieces out.

"Here, pull up hard on this one. Wait until the wheels hit a joint in the track." The two men waited until they hit a joint and then pulled. The board came up.

"*Gut!* Now this one."

Again, the two men waited until they hit a joint and then jerked. This time, an even bigger piece came out. Three more times they waited and pulled, waited, and pulled. Gerd looked at their handiwork. There was a large hole, big enough for even Joshua to crawl through, torn in the floor.

"*Sehr gut,* Gerd. The Lord is with us. Now we must pray the train will stop one more time before we get to the camp."

Gerd hesitated.

Throughout all of this, I have not even asked you for help, and now a Jew reminds me ...

Gerd bowed his head. "*Du leiber Gott.* We ask you to stop the train one more time so we may escape."

"And we ask it in the name of *Yeshua Hamashiach,*" whispered Joshua.

Gerd started to ask him who that was when there was a blast on the whistle and the train slowed.

"Thank you, Lord," whispered Joshua. "Gerd, wake Emily!"

Gerd shook Emily awake. "What, Gerd ...?" but Gerd put his hand on her lips.

"Shhh, Emily. Make no sound," he whispered. "We are going. You must be silent and do as I say. Joshua has found a way for us."

The train came to a halt. Gerd could hear the SS guards gathering on the door side of the train. Joshua grabbed his arm. "Now, Gerd. Climb through and help Emily. Roll to the dark side of the train and then head for the nearest cover you can see. Just get away. I will be right behind you."

Gerd swung his legs over the edge, and Joshua lowered him until his feet touched the gravel bed. Emily came right behind, and he lifted her down. They rolled away from the light and stood up once they were out from under the train.

"This way, Gerd." Joshua's voice almost pushed them in the dark. His hands were powerful on them as he guided them toward a clump of trees. They slid down the bank and crawled into the tall grass under the branches and lay there for a moment. They could see the legs of the prisoners as they climbed out on the other side of the train. Commanders shouted orders as the soldiers lined up all the prisoners. Gerd caught his breath and started to get up when there was a burst of machine gun fire. Joshua grabbed him and pulled him back down. All up and down the line of train cars, machine guns burst into action. Gerd could hear the people screaming, see them falling. Emily gasped and put her hands over her face. Joshua held them both down.

"Do not move, or we will meet the same fate."

In a few moments there was silence, broken by an occasional moan followed by the quick bark of a pistol. A light rain fell, muffling the gunshots.

Emily sobbed. "They were never taking us to the camp. They were bringing us here to kill us."

Joshua nodded his head behind them. "We must get further into the trees and run. We have to get as far away as we can."

They wiggled backward through the grass and the low-hanging branches until they could not see the train. Then they stood and ran through the woods.

AFTER AN HOUR, they came out of the woods into a clearing. The rain had ceased, and the moon had come out from behind the clouds. Gerd saw a building looming up in front of them. In the moonlight, he could see it was a barn—the door hung on one hinge and there were holes in the shingled roof. Joshua motioned for Gerd and Emily to stay. He crept forward across the clearing until he reached the side of the barn. Gerd watched as Joshua peeked over the sill of an open window and then ducked down. Once more he raised his head, but this time he stayed up and motioned for Gerd and Emily to come. They crossed the clearing and stood looking into the barn.

Joshua motioned toward the door. "The barn is empty. We can rest here for a while, but not too long. I don't think the guards would have noticed we were missing, but you never know. And there are plenty of other soldiers around, so we have to keep moving."

Gerd pushed the door open, and they went inside. There was a large mound of hay, and Emily sank down into it. Joshua placed his coat over her, and in a moment, she was asleep. The two men looked around the barn. On a shelf in the back, Gerd found several candles and some matches. The matches were old, but at last, he got one to ignite and lit a candle. He held the candle up and looked around. Out of the darkness, a hand pulled his arm down. "Be careful with the light, Gerd. We don't know where we are or who could be watching."

Together, the two men searched the barn. In a bin in the back, they found some dried ears of corn, but the real treasure was a cache of canned goods they found hidden in a tool chest.

Joshua held up the cans of stew and vegetables. "Someone did not enjoy being forced by the Nazis to cook an *Eintopf* every Sunday and give the savings from their one-pot meal to charity. Better for us. But we need something to open it."

Gerd reached into his pocket and pulled out a small clasp knife. "Glauss was so angry after I hit him he did not search me." He took a can, punched a hole in the lid and widened it until he could get the contents out. "Come, let's wake Emily and eat. Then we must go."

"Where will we go, Gerd?"

"We return to Ixheim, get my mother and sneak into France."

"That's your plan?"

"If you have better, tell me."

Joshua shrugged. "I guess that's the plan."

Gerd went over to Emily and roused her. The three fugitives sat on the floor and shared a small meal.

Joshua handed them each two ears of corn. "Take the dried corn in your pocket. You can suck on the kernels, and they will soften."

After they finished, Emily spoke to Joshua. "On the train, you said you had found your Messiah. What did you mean?"

Gerd nodded. "Yes, and you prayed in the name of Yeshua Hama... Hama..."

"*Yeshua Hamashiach,*" said Joshua.

The words puzzled Gerd. "Who is that?"

Joshua smiled and reached into his pocket. He pulled out a folded piece of paper and spread it open. "Let me read you something." He peered at the paper. "Who hath believed our report? And to whom is the arm of the Lord revealed? For he shall grow up before him as a tender plant, and as a root out of a dry ground: he hath no form, nor comeliness; and when we shall see him, there is no beauty that we should desire him. He is despised and rejected of men; a man of sorrows and acquainted with grief: and we hid as it were our faces from him; he was despised, and we esteemed him not."

Gerd stopped him. "I have heard this Scripture. It is from Isaiah."

Emily shook her head. "I know Isaiah well; this is not from Isaiah."

Joshua smiled at Emily. "Yes, Emily, it is. It is Isaiah, chapter fifty-three."

Emily frowned. "But I know Isaiah, and I have never heard this."

"That, my dear, is because your rabbi never read it in the

synagogue. Chapter fifty-three is called the forbidden chapter. When they come to Isaiah 52:13, they end the service. The next *Shabbat* they start at Isaiah 54."

Gerd looked at Emily. There was a strange expression on her face he could not read.

"But why?" she said.

"Because, Emily, it tells us who our Messiah is."

"What?"

"Yes, I was like you. I was waiting for Messiah. When I was in prison, they put me in a cell with a pastor from the Confessing Church. He shared this with me and wrote the words on this paper. When I heard, and he explained it to me, I knew that I, along with all of Israel, had missed a Messiah who was right before our eyes. Now, I carry this with me always. Listen and tell me who you think this describes." He continued. "Surely he hath borne our griefs, and carried our sorrows: yet we did esteem him stricken, smitten of God, and afflicted. But he was wounded for our transgressions, he was bruised for our iniquities: the chastisement of our peace was upon him; and with his stripes we are healed."

Gerd felt something like a shock run down his spine.

No one ever explained this to me.

Joshua went on. "All we like sheep have gone astray; we have turned every one to his own way; and the Lord hath laid on him the iniquity of us all. He was oppressed, and he was afflicted, yet he opened not his mouth: he is brought as a lamb to the slaughter, and as a sheep before her shearers is dumb, so he openeth not his mouth. He was taken from prison and from judgment: and who shall declare his generation? For he was cut off out of the land of the living: for the transgression of my people was he stricken. And he made his grave with the wicked, and with the rich in his death; because he had done no violence, neither was any deceit in his mouth."

A light was dawning in Gerd's heart. "But this describes Jesus Christ, his suffering, and his death. I have never seen this before."

Emily frowned. "You said this Jesus claimed to be one with God. That cannot be! It is blasphemy. Our Rabbi called Jesus, Yeshu, the Christian."

Joshua nodded. "Yes, Emily, but he was not a Christian; he was a Jew. There were no 'Christians' before 300 AD. He is Jesus the Messiah, *Yeshua Hamashiach*."

Gerd remembered a verse. "I am not sent but unto the lost sheep of the house of Israel."

"Yes," said Joshua. "God sent him to the House of Israel. He was their Messiah. In Daniel chapter nine, it is very clear the Messiah would ride into Jerusalem before they destroyed the second Temple and suffer death. That had to happen before 70 AD. Only Jesus fits."

Emily cocked her head. "Is there more?"

Joshua smiled and read on. "Yet it pleased the Lord to bruise him; he hath put him to grief: when thou shalt make his soul an offering for sin, he shall see his seed, he shall prolong his days, and the pleasure of the Lord shall prosper in his hand. He shall see of the travail of his soul, and shall be satisfied: by his knowledge shall my righteous servant justify many; for he shall bear their iniquities. Therefore will I divide him a portion with the great, and he shall divide the spoil with the strong; because he hath poured out his soul unto death: and he was numbered with the transgressors; and he bare the sin of many and made intercession for the transgressors."

Gerd stared at Joshua.

Seeing then that you have a great high priest, that is passed into the heavens, come unto God by him, seeing he ever liveth to make intercession for you, Gerd ...

"What?"

Joshua looked up. "I said nothing, Gerd."

Then from outside, they heard a truck rumbling up the road.

"It is the Nazis," cried Emily.

"Someone saw our candle and told them," said Joshua.

The three fugitives jumped to their feet. The sound of the truck grew louder ...

HEAR OH ISRAEL

*H*ear, Oh Israel

The roar of the truck grew louder. Emily grabbed Gerd's arm. "What must we do, Gerd?"

Joshua took the two of them by the arms and dragged them to the back of the barn, where there was a small door. "I will go out the front. When you hear them give chase, go out the back as quickly as you can. Run like the wind."

Gerd shook his head. "No, Joshua, I cannot leave you. They will kill you."

"And if you stay, they will kill you too, and Emily and Adina."

"Adina?"

"Your little girl. I have no one. My wife and children are gone. I have only *Yeshua*, and I will go with him." He handed Gerd the folded piece of paper. "Take this and go!"

Joshua went to the barn door and waited until he heard the truck slowing. He turned and smiled. His broken face was beautiful to Gerd. Joshua raised his hand. "The Lord bless you and keep you; the Lord make his face to shine upon you and be gracious to you; the Lord lift up his countenance upon you and give you peace." And then he was gone.

They heard someone outside shout. "*Halten! Stoppen Sie. Hände hoch.*"

Gerd opened the back door. No one was there. "Come, Emily, run!"

Together, they ran out the back toward the woods. In the distance, they heard shouts and the sound of many running feet. Then there was a shot ... another ... then a burst of shots ... then ... silence.

GERD RAN WITH EMILY, not knowing where they were going, not caring. Tears streamed down his face. They burst through a tangle of brush and onto a road. "Which way, Gerd?" Emily whispered.

"West. I think it is this way." Gerd led her down the road. In about fifteen minutes, they came to a farmhouse. A box truck stood on the road in front of the house. An old man was loading some bags from a cart into the back. They tried to walk past, but he called out. "Are you lost?"

Gerd hesitated, but Emily answered. "Yes. We were on a motor trip, but we followed the wrong road. Our car broke down. We left it down the road and are trying to find a town ..."

The old man stopped what he was doing and walked over. He looked at them for a long moment and smiled. "Not a likely story, *jünge Dame*. Perhaps you are lost in another way—from the Nazis, maybe? I saw them driving by."

Gerd's heart leaped, and he looked around for a way to escape. The old man put his hand on Gerd's arm. "Do not be afraid. No one in this entire area hates the Nazis more than I do. How can I help?"

Gerd looked at Emily. "We need to get to Ixheim."

The old man laughed. "*Gott ist gut.* I am taking this feed to Saarbrücken. I go right through Zweibrücken. I can drop you outside town, and you can walk to the village." He nodded toward the back of the truck. "Why don't you ride in the back? There's a pile of hay and your ..."

"My wife," Gerd said.

The old man smiled. "Your wife can sleep in the hay."

Gerd hesitated, but the old man pushed them toward the truck. "If you walk, they will catch you. If they don't, it will still take you two days to get where you are going. Don't worry. I will get you there safely."

Emily took the old man's hand. "How can we thank you?"

"Get away from the Nazis."

EMILY LAY in Gerd's arms as the truck rumbled down the road. Gerd glanced down and saw tears running down her face. "Joshua?"

"Yes. He gave his life so we could live. He disgusted me when I saw him on the train platform. He smelled, and his face was so ugly. I did not even recognize him, though I saw him many times in Munich."

He hath no form nor comeliness; and when we shall see him, there is no beauty that we should desire him ...

"What?"

"I said nothing, Gerd."

"Wait." Gerd reached into his pocket and pulled out the piece of paper. "Listen to this, Emily." He read. "He hath no form nor comeliness; and when we shall see him, there is no beauty that we should desire him. He is despised and rejected of men; a man of sorrows, and acquainted with grief: and we hid as it were our faces from him; he was despised, and we esteemed him not."

"Joshua disgusted me when I saw him. I turned away, I ... despised him, Emily. And yet ..."

Emily took the paper. "Surely he has borne our griefs and

carried our sorrows. He was wounded for our transgressions, he was bruised for our iniquities; the chastisement of our peace was upon him and ..." Emily wept.

Gerd finished. "... And by his stripes we are healed."

Emily looked up. "Do you know what the Hebrew pronunciation of Joshua is, Gerd?"

"No."

"Yeshua. Joshua's name in Hebrew is *Yeshua*."

The words struck Gerd's mind like a blinding light. "Emily. *Du leiber Gott* sent a Jewish man named Yeshua to die for us. We despised him when we saw him, but it did not matter to him. He sacrificed himself so that we might live."

"*Gott* sent him? But why?"

Gerd pulled Emily closer. "All my life, I have tried to obey the rules. First, my father's rules, and when I was older, the *Ordnung*. I thought my obedience would give me right standing with God. I thought being Amish was my ticket to heaven. But it was not. I did not have peace or joy in my life, at least not until I met you. But being with you did not solve my problems either, and we found ourselves in a desperate situation. Ever since I met you, *Gott* was trying to get our attention."

Emily nodded her head slowly. She looked up at her husband. "I was the same as you, Gerd. I learned the Law of Moses from my mother, but though I knew it, I could not live it. I flung myself into the things of the world—dancing, entertainment, education ..."

"The night you showed me the menorah, Emily, I heard his voice. He said, 'I am the light of the world.' This Jesus, whom I have always seen as a stern judge, relentless in his criticism, was waiting for me always with grace and mercy extended. And he was waiting for you."

"Is it ... could it be ...?"

"Yes, Emily. That is why *Gott* sent Joshua to us—to show us that Jesus is your Messiah—and mine."

Hours later, they stopped. The old man came around and opened the canvas flap covering the back. "We are outside Zweibrücken. The way is clear. Go with Gott."

Gerd helped Emily down and led her off the road onto a familiar path. It was dark when they reached the village, and Gerd could see a light burning in Christian's window. A woman came to the window and glanced out.

Hilda!

Gerd turned to Emily. "Wait here."

"Where are you going?"

"I have some unfinished business with Christian and ..."

"Hilda?"

"Yes."

"I am coming with you."

Gerd nodded. They went to the door, and Gerd pushed inside. Christian saw him and rose from his chair, his face pale. Hilda saw the look on Christian's face and turned. She threw her hands up and scrambled behind Christian. "Gerd! What are you doing here?"

Gerd walked into the room. There was no one else there. "Where is my *Mütter?*"

Christian pointed. "Still at your house."

Hilda was shaking. Her face was bloodless. "Don't kill me, Gerd. Heinrich plied me with wine and I ..."

"Heinrich? You mean the fat little man who thinks he is *Gott?* You make me sick, Hilda. You have sold yourself, and you betrayed me for what? Thirty pieces of silver?" Hilda backed up as he approached. "No, Gerd ..."

Emily came behind Gerd and took his arm. "No, Gerd."

Gerd shook his head. "No, I will not hurt her. She deserves to die, but I will forgive her." He turned to Hilda, whose mouth was gaping open. "Yes, Hilda, I forgive you. Not because you deserve it, but because my Messiah commands me."

"Your Messiah?" Christian asked.

"Yes, Christian, my Messiah. His name is Jesus. For Emily, he is *Yeshua Hamashiach.*"

"Yes, of course, Jesus. He is the Savior."

"No, Christian. You do not know him as the Savior. You know the *Ordnung* as the Savior. All your life you have believed and taught that besides accepting Jesus, one must also repent and reform their life as a separate and additional requirement to attain eternal life."

"Yes, Gerd, that is the truth."

"No, Christian, it is not. There are no additional requirements. 'Believe on the Lord Jesus Christ, that he rose from the dead and you shall be saved.' Don't you understand?"

"But we need the *Ordnung.*"

"As a roadmap, perhaps, a guide. But it is not the light. He is the light. He always was and he always will be."

Christian stared at Gerd, his mouth open. At last he whispered. "What will you do, Gerd? The Nazis will find you."

"I am taking my wife and my mother, and we are going into the West. After tonight, you will never see us again. You can stay here and wallow in your racial superiority with this Nazi filth, but you will never find the Kingdom if you believe Herr Hitler is the king."

Christian stood. "Please, Gerd. Don't leave. I am an old man. There is no one to take my place. If you go..."

"And under what conditions could I stay?"

"You must put away this woman, repent, and return to the fold. We will forgive you, and all will be well again."

"What, and marry her?" Gerd nodded at Hilda.

"Yes, or whomever, just as long as they are Amish."

Gerd stared at Christian for a long moment. He shook his head. "No, I will never do that. You see, Christian, in the end it's a

grace issue. God sent his Son and through him bestowed his infi-
nite, amazing grace on us. By grace we are saved, and that
through faith. And yet you, with your conditions and rules and
hardened heart, would take the grace away, and it would be
amazing no more. No, Christian. I go where perhaps I can see
grace at work again. I know it is not here." He turned to go but
then turned back and pointed to Hilda. "You will keep her here. If
she makes a sound or tries to leave before I am gone, I will forget
my words."

Christian nodded.

Gerd took Emily's hand. "*Kumm mit mir, Frau.*"

They turned and walked into the night.

AMERICA

our months later in early 1937, with no hope for someone to carry on as elder, the Ixheim Amish and the Ersntweiller Mennonites met and agreed to merge and establish a single congregation called Mennonitengemeinde Zweibrücken, the Mennonite Community of Zweibrücken, and the last Amish congregation in Europe ceased to exist. Gerd and Emily escaped to France with Magda, and in the spring of 1937, Emily gave birth to Adina Hirschberg. Three years later, in the summer of 1940, Gerd and Emily Hirschberg, their daughter, Adina, and Gerd's mother, Magda, came to the San Luis Valley in southern Colorado ...

GERD PULLED off the road to watch a blood-red sun sinking behind the mountains, mountains that touched the sky.

"You see, Gerd, the mountains ..."

"*Ja*, Emily, just as you said. And look. There are the cowboys."

A group of men on horseback herded a band of small, wild-looking horses toward them. Gerd stood on the running board of their truck and watched the horses as they walked. Though small, he could see the strength in them. Their leader, a power-ful-looking red stallion, nipped at the mares, reared up and whis-tled a challenge. As he watched, enthralled, a man rode up to the truck on a rangy sorrel horse.

"Howdy, stranger. I can see from your truck that you're moving. Coming here?"

"*Ja,* I will purchase the Anderson ranch."

"That's a nice piece, partner. My place is just over that hill." The tall man leaned down. "Billy Roberts."

Gerd took his hand. "Gerd Hirschberg. A pleasure to meet."

"Say, are you German?"

Gerd nodded.

"I guessed by your accent. Some of your folks have a village near here. Nice people and good farmers. They call themselves Amish." Billy pronounced it 'Aaymish.'

Gerd looked in at his mother. "The Amish are here, *Mütti.* Well, perhaps they are not as unforgiving as those in Ixheim. Maybe you will have friends in this valley."

"We'll see, Gerd, we'll see. *Ja?*"

Billy's horse nickered, and Gerd thought of Gunnar.

"You going to farm?"

Gerd turned back to the cowboy and smiled. "*Nein,* no farm-ing. We will raise fine horses."

Billy smiled. "Wal, ya come to the right place."

Gerd pointed at the herd. "Maybe horses like those. What are they?"

"Those are Mustangs. They may be little, but they are the toughest critters on four legs. They can go for days without water and bring a dead man home out of the desert."

Gerd laughed. He opened the door, took Emily by the hand and helped her out of the truck. Gerd and Emily walked together into the tall grass beside the road and looked at the land that spread before him. An evening zephyr rippled the prairie and moved away over a rise.

"Look, Gerd. It is like the ocean."

"We will put our roots down in this place, Emily. I will be a cowboy, and we will raise these Moostang horses and also a fine family."

He chuckled as Emily blushed.

"And we will put your menorah on our mantel, my wife. It will remind us that Yeshua is the light of the world, and that his light has guided us to this place. And at Christmas we will light the *menorat Hanukkah*, and we will remember your people and think of the Jewish men who gave their lives so we might live."

THE END

Chapter Four

AWAKENING

*J*ürgen closed the binder and looked over at Abigail. She was staring at the fire. Finally, she spoke. "What an incredible story, Mr. Hirschberg. I had no idea."

Jürgen nodded. "I read you this story so you might see what real oppression looks like. During World War II, the Nazis sent over five million of our people to the camps. The Jews call it The Holocaust."

"Tommy never told me about that."

"Well, it didn't fit into his worldview, now did it?" He saw the question in her eyes. "Here's what I would suggest, young lady. There's an excellent library in town, and it has access to the internet. Go do some of your own research. Look up the history of the Jews on that piece of land the anti-Semites call Palestine. See if you can find some articles about what really goes on in Israel. I think you will be very surprised."

Abigail nodded. "I can see I might." She hesitated. "But, Mr. Hirschberg, I don't know how long I will be here. I must get back to California somehow. I can't just take advantage of your kindness forever."

Jürgen shook his head. "There's nobody there for you. Where will you go?"

Abigail looked down. "I don't know." A whisper.

Jürgen pulled out his pipe. "I've been thinking about that. I talked to my friends at the restaurant in town, and they will have an opening for a waitress in the spring, when the tourist season starts. I'm thinking you might like to park here until then. Maybe get your life sorted out. Think about what you want to do with it."

Abigail looked up, her eyes wide. "Really, Mr. Hirschberg? But you don't even know me very well. And I've made such a mess of my life."

Jürgen chuckled. "I told you when we met my papa taught me how to read people. And I've been reading you. Underneath all that worldly-wise you put on, I see a nice young lady—who's kind of lost her way. We all get suckered, but that doesn't make us bad people, just foolish. You can look at your mistakes and learn from them. And I've decided I like you. So, what say you?"

"Oh, Mr. Hirschberg! I don't know what to say."

"Just say yes. And I think it's time you started calling me Uncle Jürgen."

Abigail looked at her uncle and then put her face in her hands and cried. "Why are you so kind to me?"

"I figure you need a little kindness in your life." He paused and smiled. "But you'll still have to help out around here."

"Oh, I will, I promise... Uncle Jürgen."

Jürgen decided he liked that.

Abigail composed herself. "I... I have another question, Uncle Jürgen. About the story."

"Shoot."

"Well, Gerd and Emily both became Christians. I thought the Amish were already Christians."

Jürgen was silent for a minute. "I suppose you guessed I'm a Christian?"

"Well,... I was thinking along those lines, yes."

"Just so you know, Abigail, I'm not a Christian because my parents were Amish or Jewish. I'm a Christian by choice."

"But didn't being Amish or Jewish have something to do with it?"

Jürgen chuckled. "Not really. In fact, being Amish or Jewish often can be a hindrance to becoming a Christian."

"How so, Mr. Hirschberg?"

"In some ways, the Amish and the Jews are very much alike. The Jews follow the Law of Moses, and the Amish follow the *Ordnüng*. Both are what I call 'rules for holy living.' Moses wrote one set of rules in the Pentateuch, which became the first five books of the Bible, and the Amish passed the *Ordnüng* down by word of mouth. But they both serve the same purpose. The people who follow them believe that if they keep the rules, it will give them right standing with God, make them righteous in His sight. But that's not the way. You see, the Bible tells us that the righteous live by faith. You must believe that God is who He says He is and what He says is true. So, to become a Christian, a follower of Jesus, there's only one thing you can do—believe what God said about His Son being the only remedy for our condition. And that's what Gerd and Emily did."

Abigail knit her brow. "What's our 'condition?' What does that mean?"

Jürgen looked at the grandfather clock in the corner. "Well, girl, that's a whole 'nuther conversation. What say we take it up another time? But now, we'll be burning daylight before we know it."

Abigail looked at the clock. It was midnight. "Oh, my goodness! You're right. 4:30 a.m. comes quickly around here. I should go to bed. But will you promise me we will continue this conversation?"

Jürgen nodded. "Yes, ma'am."

"Good. I'm sure I will have a lot more questions. And thank you again, Uncle."

ABIGAIL HARRIS HAD BEEN WORKING for Jürgen for a month. In that time, she had been into town twice to visit the library. She spent several hours each time doing the research Jürgen had suggested, and it had turned her world upside down. She was coming back from her second visit on the bus, lost in thought.

How could I have been so gullible? I just believed everything Tommy told me. I never asked questions!

Someone slid into the seat next to her, but she didn't look up.

"In another world?"

Startled, she turned. Johan was sitting there. He had a couple of paper bags in his arms.

"My goodness, do you always come out of nowhere?"

"Seems like I do with you. I don't mean to."

Abigail looked around. The bus was half full. "What are you doing here?"

"I was in town, working for Mr. Jarvis at the hardware store. I help him out from time to time, when things are slow at Jürgen's place. And I had to get some things for my *maam* for Thanksgiving." He pointed at the bags.

"Thanksgiving? Is it that time already?"

Johan grinned. "Four days from now."

Abigail shook her head. "I guess I have been in another world."

"My *maam* wanted me to make sure you are coming to dinner with Jürgen."

Abigail looked at Johan in surprise. "Me? But I'm a stranger. Thanksgiving is about family. I don't know, Johan... I would feel out of place."

"Well, then you can sit by me." He smiled again. "I really hope you will say yes. You have never had Thanksgiving dinner until you've had an Amish Thanksgiving. Turkey and dressing, mashed potatoes and gravy, sweet potato casserole, broccoli salad, home-made dinner rolls, apple pie, pecan pie..."

Abigail laughed. "Okay, okay, I'll come. It sounds wonderful."

Johan looked away. "Good. I'm glad. *Es wird gut sein, Sie dort zu haben.*"

He saw the puzzled look and smiled. "It will be good to have you there."

And then Abigail did something she hadn't done in a long time. She blushed.

THANKSGIVING DAY with Johan's family was like nothing Abigail had ever experienced. It was wonderful. On Thanksgiving morning, Abigail awoke early with a great sense of excitement. She dressed quickly and went down to help Jürgen feed the animals.

"Farm doesn't stop for Thanksgiving," Jürgen said as they worked together in the chill November morning.

Then at about eleven, they drove over to the Eicher farm. Abigail felt shy when they arrived, but Johan's family received her with warmth and grace, and soon she felt right at home. Johan had a large family with four older brothers and two sisters. His father was a tall, quiet man with friendly eyes, who welcomed Abigail warmly. She particularly liked Emma, Johan's youngest sister, who noticed Abigail's discomfort when she arrived and took her right under her wing. After a round of introductions, Emma took Abigail into the kitchen, where the women were cooking while discussing family news and recipes. Delicious smells that made Abigail's mouth water filled the room. Maggie greeted Abigail warmly with a hug.

"*Ich bin so froh, dass du gekommen bist*, Abigail. I am so glad you came." She turned to the other women. "Ladies, this is Abigail. I'm sure you've heard about her. She is Jürgen's niece." The women all greeted her. Emma sat her down on a stool.

Abigail pulled Emma's sleeve. "Can't I do anything to help? I can peel potatoes pretty good."

Emma grinned. "Okay. But remember, you asked for it." Emma grabbed an apron off a peg, handed it to Abigail, and then brought over an enormous bowl of potatoes and two peelers. They set the bowl on the counter in front of them and started peeling. In about twenty minutes they had the potatoes finished, and one of the other ladies whisked them off to a big pot of boiling water.

Abigail looked around. "This is wonderful, Emma. Everyone is so friendly."

Just then, Jürgen poked his head in the kitchen door. He spied Abigail and grinned. "So, Maggie the slave-driver corralled you into working, did she?"

Maggie shook her wooden spoon at Jürgen. "You old geezer! Go on back to the front room and talk about horses or hunting or whatever you men do, and leave us alone. We have serious work here, and we don't need any troublemakers."

Abigail waved her potato peeler. "Besides, Uncle Jürgen, I volunteered."

"A likely story," Jürgen grunted as he went back to the front room.

Soon it was time for the meal. Johan had not been kidding when he told Abigail she had never had Thanksgiving dinner until she'd had an Amish Thanksgiving. They sat down to eat around two o'clock. First came the salads, then the sweet potato casserole, and then the magnificent turkey with mashed potatoes, gravy, and Amish bread stuffing. Abigail ate until she thought she would burst. Thankfully, the meal was long and lingering, filled with conversation and laughter. Abigail sat between Johan and her uncle, and they would occasionally fill her in with details on Amish life.

Finally, after an enormous slice of pecan pie, Abigail had to wave off any more food. The women got up and began clearing the table while the men went outside. Abigail pitched in washing dishes, and Emma stood beside her, drying.

"So, what did you find that was different about an Amish Thanksgiving?"

Abigail thought for a moment. "First, no football, and no TV. I loved that. You all just talked about family and community and the harvest. We didn't spend the day watching parades and the NFL."

"What else?"

"All the food was from your farms or gardens, not from the supermarket. And it wasn't hectic. Nobody had to run to the airport to pick someone up, and the entire focus was being together here, in this house. It was lovely, Emma."

Just then, Johan stuck his head in the door. "Hey, Emma, can I liberate Abigail and show her the farm?"

Emma giggled. "That's his code. It means he wants to go out walking with you."

Abigail went to the coatroom to get her jacket. She passed her uncle, who was sound asleep in a chair in front of the fire.

Johan smiled. "Naps are also a popular and well-deserved activity after Thanksgiving. My *maam* and several of the ladies are upstairs taking a *Mittagsschlaf.* That's 'afternoon nap' in case you didn't guess."

It was a brisk fall afternoon. The Eicher farm was orderly, with several large red outbuildings. Chickens scratched in the yard. Abigail heard cows lowing in the distance. She pulled her jacket closed against the chill breeze. In the distance, a row of aspen trees showed off their fall colors of red and gold. Johan led her to a small stock pond. Two enormous cottonwood trees dominated the scene, their leaves golden against a wonderful mountain backdrop.

"It's beautiful here, Johan."

"*Ja, es ist ein wunderbarer Ort.*"

Abigail glanced at him.

"That means, 'Yes, it is a wonderful place.'" He was silent for a moment. "Do you know what your plans are?" He hesitated when he saw the troubled expression on her face. "Sorry, I... I don't mean to pry."

"Oh, you're not, but it is something that has been on my mind a lot. For now, I've decided to stay for at least a while. Uncle Jürgen found me a job waitressing in town, starting in the spring, if I stay. In the meantime, he's invited me to stay on with him until I know more about what I want. So, I have some options. I'm going to take the time until then to get my life sorted out. You know, figure out what I'm going to do with myself."

He smiled. *"Das ist gut."*

She was silent for a long moment. "You know little about me, but I made some bad choices and got myself headed down a hard path. I'm hoping to change that."

"We all make wrong choices, sometime." He looked away and was quiet for a moment. Then he steered the conversation away. "What do you like to do? I mean really like?"

She thought for a moment. "I love to write. I've always kept a journal, and I've been writing stories since I was in the second grade. But I never went to college, at least full-time. I took a few classes at the junior college in Tarzana. Maybe someday..."

Johan nodded. "You know, there's a very good college, Adams State University, right in Alamosa. I believe they have night and weekend classes. You could start there. Maybe that's something you might think about, that is... if... well, if you're going to stay longer..."

Abigail looked up at Johan.

And that's the big question of my life, isn't it? Am I going to stay?

Chapter Five

A NEW BEGINNING

$\mathcal{W}$inter came to the San Luis Valley of Colorado. Abigail, growing up in Los Angeles, had never experienced snowstorms or deep snow before. It took some getting used to, but soon she loved the pristine whiteness, the beautiful snowcapped peaks that surrounded the Alamosa ranch, and the brisk winter air that turned her cheeks red and compelled her to finish her tasks quickly.

There was something else that made her cheeks red, and that was whenever Johan came to help her clear snow away from the barn doors, or clean the stalls. She dropped by where he was working, taking him hot coffee in a thermos, or sometimes sneaking a fresh hot bun out of Maggie's kitchen.

Johan's inherent manliness drew her like a magnet. He was a what-you-see-is-what-you-get young man—respectful, kind, and yet strong, focused, and hard-working... besides being very good-looking. Yes, Johan distracted Abigail almost to the point of confusion, and one night she sat down with Jürgen and opened her heart. They had finished with the dinner dishes, and then Jürgen patted her on the shoulder.

"Something on your mind, girl?"

"What makes you ask, Uncle Jürgen?"

"Well, you've been quiet lately, lost in thought."

Abigail nodded. "It's been that obvious?"

Jürgen smiled. "*Ja*, pretty obvious. Want to talk about it?"

Abigail hung up her dish towel and slipped off her apron. "Okay."

They got some coffee from the pot and went into the front room. The fire had died down, so Jürgen put a couple of logs on it. They sat on the couch in front of the fire and enjoyed the blaze for a few minutes.

"So, you're wondering what to do with your life, and what to do with your feelings for Johan." It wasn't a question, but a statement.

Abigail looked at Jürgen and felt her face get hot. "How did you know about Johan, Uncle Jürgen?"

"Oh girl, it don't take but one eye and half a brain to see you get all fluttery whenever that boy shows up."

Abigail looked down at the floor. "That obvious, huh?"

"Don't make me no nevermind, girl, you can't help the way you feel."

"But he's Amish, Uncle Jürgen, and I'm, well, I'm kind of damaged goods and about as far away from going to church as a girl can get. I just can't figure out how I got this far off track."

"Do you like him?"

Abigail felt the flush creeping up her face... again. "Well,... yes, I like him very much. He's a real man, and he treats me with kindness and respect."

"Oh, I think he feels more than that for you, Abigail."

"But, Uncle Jürgen, that's not good. I am not the girl that Johan needs. He needs a nice Amish girl, someone who has the same values that he has. He doesn't need someone who's used up and tossed aside like a piece of trash." Abigail sat for a moment... and then put her face in her hands and cried. "I'm not... I mean I lived with Tommy, I let him, you know... Oh, Uncle Jürgen, I am used and damaged goods. No man would want me, no real man, anyway. A leopard can't change its spots. I think I should just go away." The tears fell faster.

Jürgen reached over and pulled Abigail against his shoulder. She buried her head against him and sobbed. Jürgen patted her shoulder gently. "There now, girl, you got a pretty low opinion of yourself, but I'm afraid it don't match up with what everybody 'round here sees in you. And I know the good Lord is just waitin' for the chance to talk to you about all this. I reckon that Mr. Tommy just came along when you were vulnerable and showed you a handful of gimme and a mouthful of much obliged." He reached into the drawer in the little coffee table in front of the couch and pulled out a packet of tissues. He pressed one into Abigail's hand.

She lifted her head, wiped her eyes, and blew her nose. "You know me pretty well already, Uncle Jürgen." She wiped her eyes again. "Yes, you're right. I was very vulnerable when I met Tommy. A car wreck killed my mom when I was seventeen, and my dad left me with his parents and went to Venezuela to work in the oil fields. Six months later, a derrick accident killed him. After that, I felt really lost. I was casting about for something to do with my life, and a friend suggested I take a political science class at the local junior college. Tommy was the TA, the teaching assistant in the class, and he did the lectures when the professor was away, which was often."

Jürgen nodded. "And he seemed like a real smart guy, no doubt."

Abigail nodded. "He was smart and well-read, and he was a wonderful speaker. At first, I didn't understand all the things he was talking about, but after a few classes, what he was saying sounded good. He talked about the poor oppressed people and how the capitalists and land-owners took advantage of them to get richer."

"Then he asked you out for some coffee or something."

Abigail looked at Jürgen in surprise. "How did you know that?"

Jürgen chuckled. "I may be old, but I can still spot the prettiest gal in the room. If I can, Mr. Tommy certainly could."

"So... yes, one afternoon after class, he asked me to go have coffee at the Student Union."

"You paid, right?"

"Well, he got free coffee because he was on staff. I did pay for mine."

"Should have been your first clue, Abigail." He paused... "So, he sat you down and started talkin' a blue streak. Never asked about you, what your background was, what you were interested in."

Abigail looked down. "That's right. He was so full of himself, but I felt flattered that the teacher would take an interest in me. I listened while he talked about the indigenous people of this country and how they had their land stolen by colonizers. He talked about how the founders of our country were slave owners... you know, a lot of stuff."

Jürgen shook his head. "You know, girl, there is probably some truth in what he said, but he most likely left out the important parts. Parts like how this country, despite its many flaws, has always been the freest country in the world. What he didn't say was that you don't have to be perfect to be good—that people come here from all over the world to be free. How do you think the Amish got here?"

"What do you mean, Uncle Jürgen?"

"The Anabaptists, the forerunners of the Amish, were one of the most persecuted groups in history. They read the Bible and decided they should not baptize their infants but wait for them to be old enough to decide for themselves. Well, that made the secular authorities and the religious bigwigs angry because when you baptized a baby in those days, it put them on the tax rolls. So the Anabaptists, or anti-Baptists, were taking money out of the pockets of the secular and religious powers-that-be. They started rounding up the Anabaptists and burning them at the stake."

"I never knew that."

"In the 1700s, William Penn, who owned what became the state of Pennsylvania, sent his representatives to Switzerland, Holland, and Germany, and invited the Amish to come to America. He promised them religious freedom. They came and founded the settlement at Northkill, Pennsylvania. Then they spread out into Ohio, Indiana, and Colorado. Now the Amish are in most states in this country. I bet Mr. Tommy didn't talk about religious freedom, or that we have an almost perfect form of government—a form, that if it wasn't for the men who try to use it for their own gain, should be a shining light to the world."

"Do you mean democracy, Uncle Jürgen?"

"No, the founders didn't give us democracy. They knew democracy was the worst thing you could do to a country. Democracy means the majority rules, with no safeguards for the minority. Political parties would love to have a democracy so they could impose their ideologies however they wanted, just so long as they got the most votes. No, what we have is a constitutional republic."

"What does that mean?"

"A constitutional republic is built on a constitution that guarantees the same rights to everyone, no matter who's running the government. So, the minority is always protected from the whims of the majority. Our founders wrote it after much prayer and fasting. It's a divinely inspired document and incorporates much of the teaching from the book of Leviticus."

"Leviticus?"

"That's one of the books in the Old Testament. You see, Abigail, the founders built this country on the Judeo-Christian ethic, right off the teachings of the Bible. The problem is, you must have a relationship with God to understand that."

"Tommy said that religion is the opium of the masses. That people just use it for a crutch."

"Well, he didn't actually say it. Karl Marx, the founder of communism, said it. Mr. Tommy sounds like he was one of those useful idiots who spout the communist line without having the slightest understanding of what an evil system it is. Did you know that records show over one hundred million people have died because of communist regimes, including through genocides, executions, and famines? Bet Mr. Tommy didn't tell you that."

Abigail shook her head. "No. He always said Christians were the problem."

"Sure he did, because Christianity, real Christianity, not some man-made religion, makes you take a long hard look at what a broken person you really are, right from the git-go. The book of Romans lays it out when it says, 'All have sinned and fallen short of the glory of God.' You see, to understand what Christianity is, you first need to believe that what the Bible says is true. Then, with that as your guideline, you discover God... a being Who has always been, and you find out how He created a human race He wanted to have an eternal relationship with. He designed man to live forever, and there was no death in the world. But the first man he made, Adam, decided he wanted to go his own way, and the Bible tells us that by that act, sin and death entered the world, and all mankind has been laboring under the curse of death since then. And we all have a broken nature that won't allow us to do good."

"So, is that why we make bad choices, Uncle Jürgen? Especially about what we do with our lives."

"You hit the nail on the head, girl. See, the Bible tells us that God breathed His Spirit into the man and that's what made him alive. He had a direct link to God, and God could help Him with every decision. But when Adam decided not to do what God asked, God had to remove His Spirit from Adam, and the first man lost his connection to everything that is good and pure and righteous. The light went out."

"But Tommy always said he wouldn't want a God that sends people to hell."

"God doesn't send people to hell, Abigail; they are on their way there from their first breath. You see, just like you have blonde hair and blue eyes because your mother or father did, you also acquired your inability to do good, your broken nature, from your first ancestor, Adam. Without the Spirit of God in you to give you real life and direction, you are a walking dead woman. You see, the actual definition of death is separation from God. And death is the most obvious way we know that our relationship with Him is broken."

Abigail looked at Jürgen, her eyes wide. "That makes sense, Uncle Jürgen."

"Sure it does. If you look at all the other religions and 'ways to God' you see that believing in Jesus is the only thing that makes sense. And here's the secret. God doesn't send people to hell. He provided the only way to keep them from going there, the only remedy for their 'condition.' Because the one and only thing God has on his heart is to be back in relationship with the humanity He created."

Abigail had an epiphany. "That's the condition we talked about before, isn't it, Uncle Jürgen? So, what is the remedy?"

"Simple. Because God is a just God, he must punish man's sinful behavior. But because He is a merciful God, He sent His own Son to take the punishment for every human being on this planet—past, present and future. When Jesus died on the cross, He said, 'It is finished.' What He meant was, because He was God's Son, He was fully qualified to pay the penalty for your sin and mine. And three days after He died, He rose from the dead with the power to give everyone who believed in Him the eternal life that we gave up long ago. If we believe His death, burial and resurrection is true, we can be restored to the relationship with God that He is so eager to have with us... again."

"So, God is actually involved in our lives, trying to get us to come back to Him?"

"He sure is. In fact, I'd like to read you another story. It's about how God involved Himself directly not only in my *daed* and my *grössdaddi's* lives, but in my sister Adina's life and my *maam* and *grossmütter's* lives too. You up for it?"

"Oh yes, Uncle Jürgen."

Jürgen went out and came back with another binder. "My sister Adina was a wonderful writer. This story is called 'A Light in the Window' and every bit is true."

He sat down and began to read. "Whenever I see snow, I remember the miracle..."

A LIGHT IN THE WINDOW

ADINA

*W*henever I see snow, I remember the miracle.

I remember the white flakes falling like tiny angels outside the window. I remember the flickering lamps, the wonder on my mama's face and my grandmother's whispered prayers of thanks. Yes, I remember the miracle.

I know we all have small miracles every day, because the hand of *Gott* guides each of us, and he is always doing wonderful things if only our eyes are open to see them. But this was a big miracle, and though I am old now and my failing memory hides many things from me, this miracle has never left me, shining through all the days of my life, like the Hanukkah menorah that burned in our window in the winter of 1945, tended by a little girl who was hoping and praying her papa would come home for Christmas.

In those days, I lived in Colorado with my mama, Emily, my grandmother, Magda, and my papa, Gerd. We all came to America from Germany in 1940—to the beautiful San Luis Valley. My papa bought a ranch and raised Mustang horses. After we were there for a year, Papa, Mama, and my grandmother became citizens. Then the war came to America. Because my Papa was German, he knew he could help the American cause, so he enlisted. Mama said joining up was hard for him because he was raised in the Amish faith, and he always believed violence toward other men was wrong. But he also believed he needed to help defend America from the evil that was Hitler—an evil he had seen firsthand. He became an officer and left us to go with the army. The day he went away—oh, he was so handsome in his uniform, and my mama cried.

Now the war in Europe was over, but my Papa was not home, and we had not heard from him for several months. My mama was so anxious, and I remember hearing her cry at night when she thought I could not hear her.

Back in 1936, there were bad times in Germany. My Papa was an Amish man who owned a farm in the tiny village of Ixheim, right on the border with France. He lived there with my grandmother. That was before I was born. My mother was a Jewish girl who was being hunted by the Nazis. She was trying to escape to France, but she only got as far as my Papa's barn. When my Papa found her hiding there, he fell in love with her. He married her, but the Nazis found them and sent them to the Dachau concentration camp. On the way there, they met a Jewish man who helped them escape. He also helped them to discover their Messiah, *Yeshua Hamaschiach*, Jesus Christ, but though that's another story. That is why we always had Christmas and Hanukkah at the same time in our house in Colorado. And that is where the miracle began.

When my papa and mama left Germany in 1936, my papa also left the Amish Church. The Nazis had persuaded the Amish to turn in Jews and Communists to the Gestapo, and there were other things the church did my papa could not agree with. Papa sold his farm to his friend, and my parents and my grandmother escaped over the border to France. I was born there, in the village of Épernay, outside of Paris in 1937. Papa found work in the vineyards, and mama taught in a school for Jewish refugee children. My *Mütti,* that's what I called my grandmother, stayed at home and took care of me. Though I don't remember it, *Mütti* said we lived in a little cottage in the middle of a large vineyard where they grew grapes to make French Champagne. It was very long ago, but sometimes I see a picture in my mind of a rock wall with purple and yellow flowers spilling over it and my *Mütti* sitting in the sun in an old chair.

Then things got bad in France and the French Army moved to the border to keep the Germans from getting in. My papa was very smart, and he knew all the Jewish people in France were in danger if the Germans came, so with the money he got from selling his farm, he bought tickets to America. And so, when I was three years old, we came to Colorado and bought our ranch. Then my papa went away to the war. And that's where *this* story begins.

*A*dina Hirschberg looked out the window of the front room and watched as the heavy flakes floated down from a leaden sky. As far as she could see, the fields and pastures around their ranch were covered with a deep fall of white. It had been snowing for a week, a rare occurrence in the San Luis Valley. Now it was eight days until Christmas.

The sound of her *grossmütter,* Magda, entering the room made her turn her head. Magda held an armful of wood that she laid on the hearth before the roaring fireplace.

Adina ran to her grandmother. "*Mutti, Mutti!*"

Magda turned and embraced the girl. "What is it, my Dina?"

"When will Papa be home?"

Magda shook her head. She looked over the little girl's shoulder at the snow swirling outside. "We don't know, little one. He has not sent a letter in some time."

"Will he be home by Hanukkah? By Christmas?"

Magda smiled. In the Hirschberg house, Hanukkah and Christmas happened at the same time.

Emily Hirschberg came in from the kitchen. "We are getting

low on flour and oil, Mother, and I'm worried you won't be able to make *stöllen*."

Adina's face puckered. "No *stöllen!*"

Magda smiled. "Don't worry little one. We will find some flour to make your favorite."

The little girl jumped and clapped her hands. "Oh, good!"

Emily took hold of her daughter's hand. "Run upstairs and see how the kittens are doing."

Adina ran off to play with the new kittens that their cat, Hansli, rather than face the cold in the barn, had birthed in an extra upstairs closet. Emily watched her go.

"I don't know, Magda. We have not been able to get to the store for a week. There is too much snow. Our truck can't get through it. Billy Roberts has not been by either. I'm afraid all of our neighbors are in the same predicament. Oh, I wish Gerd had not bought a ranch so far out of town." She burst into tears.

Magda took Emily in her arms. "What is it my girl? Gerd?"

Emily snuffled in the safety of Magda's shoulder and then finally raised her head. She pulled a hanky from her apron pocket and dabbed her eyes. "Yes, mother, I am so worried. I have not heard from Gerd since September, and his letters were so vague. He said even though the war was over, his duties were keeping him in Europe for some time. He said he would be coming home as soon as he could."

Emily held Magda tighter.

"Why did he have to go to the war, Magda? We were so happy."

Magda sighed and pulled her daughter-in-law closer. "It is exactly because you were so happy that he had to go. When we came to America we found a new home, good friends, and a country that accepted us just as we are. We found freedom, and that was what Gerd went to the war for. He felt that he should do something for the country that has given him so much even in the short time we have been here."

"But the Amish are against war."

Magda nodded. "Yes, we are ... for the most part."

"What do you mean?"

Magda drew Emily to the couch in front of the fire, and they sat. "I have spoken with the other Amish who live in this valley, and they tell me that many of their men have faced the same dilemma Gerd went through. I think the Amish in America have struggled with this since they first stepped ashore in Philadelphia two hundred years ago."

Magda paused and looked out at the snow. "Gerd faced this when the Nazi Glauss tried to lay hands on you. Even though our Lord Jesus tells us if we are struck on the cheek, we should turn the other cheek, there comes a time when a man must choose to defend his family and those he loves. Many Amish men have watched their families murdered before their eyes, and I am thinking that did not please the Lord."

"*Mütti!*" Emily's eyes widened.

"When you watched your mother and father being taken away and your brother killed by the Nazis, what did you feel in your heart?"

Emily looked down. "I wanted to protect them, I wanted to save them. I would have killed the Germans if I had a gun."

"I don't think those feelings are from the devil, Emily. That is why, when we left the Amish church in Ixheim, I felt free for the first time. I know the Lord wants us to be kind and gentle, to turn the other cheek if we can, but I think he also expects us to defend those he has given us to protect. That is why Gerd went. He wanted to make sure that the country that had given his wife and child a future would continue to exist in the face of great evil. That is why I gave him my blessing."

Emily looked at Magda and then sank back against her. The old woman brushed Emily's hair back and kissed her forehead. "I understand your worry for Gerd, and I am worried too. But the Lord has directed our path since the day you came to us. I am so thankful you hid in our barn, Emily, for you are truly a daughter to me."

Adina heard them talking and paused at the top of the stairs. Their words troubled her.

What if Papa can't find his way home? Maybe he's lost in the snow.

She went into the room where the kittens were. The tiny soft balls of fur were snuggled up against their mama. Hansli looked up at Adina and then yawned a big cat yawn.

"How are your babies today, Hansli?" The cat answered with a soft purr. Adina counted the kittens and made sure they were all alive. When she was satisfied, she sat on the bed. It was cold in the upstairs room even though the heat from the fireplace could spread through the well-designed ranch house. Adina pulled a down comforter around her and thought about her father. She tried to remember what he looked like, but it was hard for she was only five years old on the day he left. She did remember one thing, though. Her father, a tall man wearing brown clothing, took her in his arms and held her close. His whispered words were still with her.

"Do not worry, Adina. The Lord Yeshua will be with me, and I have asked him to watch over you and your mother and *Mütti*. That is all we can do—put our lives into his hands and trust him. I will do my best to come home to you, I promise, but if I do not, always remember that I love you so much."

Her papa had been gone for three years now. Even though she sometimes had trouble remembering exactly what his face looked like she always remembered his words. Hansli climbed out of the box, leaving her now-sleeping kittens, and climbed up on the bed. Adina pulled the cat under the comforter so that only her head was sticking out. Hansli settled down and began to purr.

"What should we do, Hansli? Why hasn't Papa come home?" She bowed her head.

"Yeshua, where is my papa? We need him to come home. Mama needs him, and I do too. Won't you help us?"

She sat silently for a long time. Suddenly an idea came to the little girl. "Hansli! I know what to do! It's almost time to start lighting the menorah for Hanukkah. We'll put it in the window instead of on the mantle. That way Papa can see it, and the light will guide him home."

Adina put Hansli on the bed and jumped up. The cat protested, but Adina was already out the door and clattering down the stairs.

"Mama! Mama! I know how to bring Papa home."

DACHAU—APRIL 1945

*G*erd Hirschberg sat in the passenger side of the Jeep with two more MIS officers in the back seat. It was April 29. He and several intelligence officers had been embedded with the 42nd Rainbow division and sent with them to liberate the Nazi concentration camp at Dachau. Behind them, a group of newspaper reporters and photographers followed in another jeep. Gerd's heart was pounding as they drove slowly toward the camp looming in front of them. He turned to one of the Intelligence officers behind him, Major Heym. The Major was a German refugee like himself. He and Gerd had gone through training at Camp Ritchie, the secret installation where American soldiers who spoke fluent German trained in interrogation and counterintelligence techniques before being sent to Europe.

"This is the camp where the Nazis sent my wife's father, Emilé Weissbach, in 1936."

Major Heym had a quizzical look. "I didn't think they were rounding up Jews so early."

Gerd shook his head. "Emilé was also a Communist, so he was one of the first to go. They took his wife with him and murdered his son Jürgen, my wife's brother."

Heym looked away. "I came from Munich. We saw what was happening, and I escaped with my wife and children in 1934. The rest of my family has disappeared. I hope that some of them fled as I did, but I am afraid they waited too long and the Nazis rounded them up and sent them to the camps."

As they drove up the road toward the main gate, the snow was still two feet deep in places, and it was cold, very cold. There was a line of railroad cars on a siding by the road. US soldiers were opening the cars, and many were stumbling away and vomiting. Gerd could see piles of human bodies inside the cars.

"*Mein Gott!*" said Heym, slipping into German. "These soldiers did not understand what we would find here."

Gerd turned his head away, his mind refusing to believe what his eyes were seeing. Even though they were briefed the previous week about what the Allied forces were discovering in the concentration camps, Gerd could not assimilate the enormity of what he was seeing. Another Jeep drove down from the gate. A colonel on the passenger side spoke to them.

"Hirschberg, Heym! We need you at the gate for translating. General Linden is waiting."

They drove to the gate and clambered out. A young man in the uniform of the Waffen SS stood surrounded by Army personnel and some reporters. His face was pale and his hands trembled. General Linden nodded to Gerd. "Captain Hirschberg. Please ask this man his name and rank. Then ask where the camp commandant is."

Gerd spoke rapidly to the German. The officer answered. Gerd translated for the General. "His name is SS 2nd Lieutenant Heinrich Wicker. The camp commandant, Martin Weiss, who fled with most of the regular guards last night, left him in charge. Lieutenant Wicker is ready to surrender the camp."

Just then the sound of tumult interrupted them. Gerd turned. Men, obviously prisoners, poured out of the barracks behind the barbed wire fence. They shouted in unison. American soldiers stood watching in dismay, many of them weeping at the sight of the horribly emaciated prisoners dragging themselves to the fence. Gerd saw several German soldiers being led away to a separate enclosure. They disappeared from sight and then shots rang out. Gerd turned to Major Heym. "What is happening, Major?"

Heym shook his head. "I think that any German soldier caught inside this camp will not leave it alive."

"But what about the Geneva Convention?"

Heym shrugged. "These Germans, these animals, have given up their rights under the Convention. I suggest you stop with the questions, Captain. We are in hell here and our men are furious. Whatever happens, these Germans have brought upon themselves."

Gerd looked back for the young man who had surrendered the camp. He had vanished along with the soldiers who had been with him . Heym shrugged. "As I said ..."

Shots rang out, and everyone ducked and ran. Gerd saw soldiers pointing at a guard tower. He saw flashes of light as whoever was in the tower fired their weapon out the window. The Americans surrounded the tower and unleashed a maelstrom of bullets into the tower. Two men pitched out of the window, and the firing stopped. Gerd watched as the Americans ran up and finished the Germans off with bursts of rifle fire.

Around the camp there were other outbursts of gunfire as some German soldiers fought to the finish rather than being shot by the Americans or torn to pieces by the prisoners. Gerd saw GIs rushing by, their faces contorted with rage and grief. Gerd shook his head.

Dear Lord! Who could even think that human beings could descend to such behavior? It is beyond belief.

THAT EVENING, Gerd sat with his commanding officer, Gen. Oscar Koch. Gerd had spent the rest of the day interrogating the few surviving German soldiers.

"What I understand from the interrogations, sir, is the Germans knew the Allies were coming and started shipping prisoners here from other camps so they would have time to exterminate them. The death train outside the camp was part of that. It arrived a week ago. When the Nazis realized they would not have time, they locked the doors and let them all die."

Koch shook his head. "Linden told me that when our boys saw what was going on here, there was a period of about half an hour when the GIs went crazy. They shot any German they saw or turned them over to the prisoners, and they were beaten to death. Awful."

Gerd looked at General Koch. "Sir, I would like to ask a favor —well, two favors."

"What's that Hirschberg?"

"First, this camp is where the Nazis sent my wife's parents in 1936. I would like permission to look at the records and speak with some Jews here to see if I can find out what happened to the Weissbachs."

"What's the second favor, Captain?"

"I would like permission to communicate with my wife and let her know where I am. She hasn't heard from me for several weeks."

Koch stood up. "The first request I will grant, Captain, since we need you to speak to as many prisoners as possible and get to the bottom of what happened here and in the other camps around Germany and Poland. I must deny the second request. This entire operation has gone top secret. We need to keep any information about it on a need to know basis. Many Nazis involved in this, like Weiss, are in hiding. They must not know what we are doing. So no communication from now on."

"But, sir, that may take months."

Koch went to the door and turned. "I'm well aware of that, but we have a lot of cleanup to do here, and you are an important but secret part of that. No letters or phone calls until further orders. Understood?"

Gerd stood and saluted. "Yes, Sir. Understood."

Koch turned and left the room. Gerd sank back down in his chair.

This is not good, Lord. Emily will be very worried.

THE MENORAH

*a*dina ran down the stairs to her mother. "Mama, Mama! I know how to bring Papa home!"

Emily pulled the child up close. "How, Dina?"

"Tonight, we light the Hanukkah menorah, right?"

Her mother looked down at Dina's eager face. "Yes, my darling girl, but ..."

"Don't you see, Mama? This year, instead of putting it on the mantle, we will put it in the window so Papa can see it and find his way home."

Emily looked away and tears formed in her eyes.

If only it were that simple ...

"Mama? I know it will work. The light in the window will be like a star to guide Papa home"

"Oh, to have the faith of a child again."

Emily turned to see Magda standing there with a smile. She turned back to Dina. "You are right, Dina. We will put the menorah in the window. And each day, we will light a new lamp, and by Christmas, there should be enough light for Papa to see all the way from Germany."

THAT NIGHT, they gathered in the living room. The fire was bright and warm. Outside, the gray light of dusk was giving way to nightfall. Emily brought the beautiful menorah from its place of honor in the hallway cabinet and placed it on the table they had moved in front of the large window. The golden lamp gleamed— its many cups and arms reflecting the light from the fire.

Emily said, "My grandfather made this *menorat Hanukkah*. He passed it down to my mother, and it is the only thing I have left to remember my father and mother by. When I was a little girl like you, Dina, we started celebrating Hanukkah on the tenth day of December. But that is because most Jewish homes have not yet seen the truth that their Messiah, Yeshua, has already come. Your papa and I know that Jews and Gentiles alike share the wonderful savior of the world. So we celebrate Hanukkah and Christmas together to remember the coming of the Light into this world."

Dina nodded. "So we are the only house in the world who does it this way, right?"

Magda laughed. "That may be true, Dina, but knowing Jesus, there may be many other Jews who have seen the truth. You just never know."

Emily pointed to a cup in the middle of the lamp stand. It was higher than the other eight cups. There was a wax candle in the cup. "This is the *Shamash,* the servant candle. It is used to kindle the other cups. That is why we use a wax candle here, so in case the other lights go out, it is ready to serve them by relighting them. Each night, we will fill another cup with oil and we will keep the menorah burning for an hour. By the end of the eighth day, all the cups will be lit."

"And the light will be so bright that Papa will see it, and it will guide him home."

Emily looked at Magda. "Yes, Dina, it will guide Papa home."

"Before we light the candle, tell me the story, Mama."

The three Hirschberg women sat together on the comfortable couch in front of the fire. Emily began. "Some twenty-one hundred years ago, the land of Israel came under the rule of the Syrian-Greek emperor Antiochus, who issued a series of decrees designed to force his pagan beliefs and rituals upon the Jewish people. He outlawed the study of Torah and observing its commands and defiled the Holy Temple in Jerusalem with Greek idols.

"A small, vastly outnumbered band of Jews waged battle against the mighty Greek armies and drove them out of the land. When they reclaimed the Holy Temple, they wished to light the Temple's menorah, only to discover the Greeks had ruined all the holy oil. All that remained was one jar of pure oil —enough to last one night—and it would take eight days to procure new, pure oil so they could keep the lamp lit day and night."

"But Yahweh gave them a miracle—the one-day supply of oil lasted eight days and nights. Ever since then, the Jews light the Hanukkah menorah on each of the eight nights of Hanukkah."

Adina turned to her grandmother. "Now the Christmas story, *Mütti!*"

Magda reached over to the table by the couch and took up the Bible lying there. She opened it. "Mary and Joseph knew the baby Mary carried in her womb was the Messiah of Israel and the entire world, for they had been told by angel messengers who came from God. Then the Emperor in Rome decreed everyone should go to their hometown to be counted in a new census so he could tax them. So Joseph took Mary to Bethlehem for the census, but *Gott* was in it, for many centuries before, the prophet Micah had foretold that the Messiah would be born in the town of David. So they came there ..."

"But they could not find a room in the inn, right *Mütti.*"

Magda smiled. "No, Dina, they could not. So Joseph found a man who let them stay in his stable. Can you imagine that the

God of the Universe chose the most humble of places to be born?"

"And then the angels came?"

Emily laughed. "Soon you will be old enough to tell the story, Dina, for you know it by heart already."

Magda opened the Bible and read. "And it came to pass in those days, that there went out a decree from Caesar Augustus that all the world should be taxed. And this taxing was first made when Cyrenius was governor of Syria. And all went to be taxed, every one into his own city. And Joseph also went up from Galilee, out of the city of Nazareth, into Judaea, unto the city of David, which is called Bethlehem; because he was of the house and lineage of David: To be taxed with Mary, his espoused wife, being great with child.

"And so it was that, while they were there, the days were accomplished that she should be delivered. And she brought forth her firstborn son, and wrapped him in swaddling clothes, and laid him in a manger; because there was no room for them in the inn.

"And there were in the same country shepherds abiding in the field, keeping watch over their flock by night. And, lo, the angel of the Lord came upon them, and the glory of the Lord shone round about them: and they were sore afraid. And the angel said unto them, "Fear not: for, behold, I bring you good tidings of great joy, which shall be to all people.

"For unto you is born this day in the city of David a Savior, which is Christ the Lord. And this shall be a sign unto you; Ye shall find the babe wrapped in swaddling clothes, lying in a manger. And suddenly there was with the angel a multitude of the heavenly host praising God, and saying, 'Glory to God in the highest, and on earth peace, good will toward men."

"And it came to pass, as the angels were gone away from them into heaven, the shepherds said one to another, Let us now go even unto Bethlehem, and see this thing which is come to pass, which the Lord hath made known unto us. And they came with haste, and found Mary, and Joseph, and the babe lying in a manger. And when they had seen it, they made known abroad the saying which was told them concerning this child. And all they that heard it wondered at those things which were told them by the shepherds."

Emily put her arm around Dina. "When Yeshua grew up, he taught the things of God to the people of Israel. But many people who were not Jews believed also. That is because God sent Jesus to everyone to tell them they did not have to live in the darkness of sin anymore. He said, 'I am the light of the world: he that followeth me shall not walk in darkness, but shall have the light of life.'"

"When your papa and I met, and I showed him the menorah, he said *Gott* spoke to him and said 'I am the light.' Then when the Nazis found us and sent us away to the concentration camp ...'"

"... That is when you met Joshua?"

"Yes, Dina, that is when we met Joshua, a Jew who knew his Messiah. He gave his life so your papa and I could escape from the Nazis. When we light the menorah, I always remember him, for not only did he save our lives, he showed us the one who gives eternal live."

"*Yeshua Hamaschiach*?"

"Yes, Dina, Jesus the Messiah."

Dina sighed. "And then you escaped and went to France, and I was born." She snuggled into her mother's arms. "Oh, Mama, how I love the stories."

Emily looked up. Night had fallen. "Come, Dina, it is time to light the menorah."

THE MARCH—MAY 1945

The man pulled the ragged coat around him. It was spring, but he was cold, always cold. His feet moved on the road, feet that no longer seemed connected to his legs. Steady now, one foot in front of the other.

I must keep moving ... if I stop, I will die ...

They had marched for three days, and today, a heavy snow had been falling since before dawn. It chilled him to the bone. Still they marched, trudging along in the snow, their naked feet turning the white into a morass of mud and blood. They kept their eyes down, so they would not make eye contact with the guards and draw their attention.

One foot in front of the other ...

He watched those who could not keep up a steady marching pace pulled out of line and shot by the guards. Others, many of them friends, collapsed and died along the side of the road.

Keep moving or you will die ...

The man looked up. The clouds were breaking, and the steady snow turned to random flakes. He wanted to end it all, just stop, let the guards take him.

So after all these years of surviving, I am to die on a muddy road in the south of Germany. Ach zo! Then I will be with you, my beloved ...

But his feet would not stop. They moved as though they had a life of their own. He looked down at the hands that were showing out of the frayed cuffs of. Once they had been powerful hands, the hands of a man in his prime, now they were the hands of a scarecrow, the skin clinging to the bones and thin as parchment paper. A small smile played over his once handsome face.

Oh my dearest, if you could see me now ...

In the days before Nazis forced them out of the camp, rumors abounded that the Americans were only hours away. Many of the guards deserted, and a spirit of hope grew among the Jews. Still, conditions were horrific, and hundreds died every day. Typhus raged. Then, early in the morning of April 26, the Nazis put many prisoners on a train. After it left, the guards came to the barracks. The old man had been told to prepare to leave. The SS troops formed up a large group of prisoners, half Jews and half Russian POWs, and marched out of the camp.

The old man had fallen in beside his friend, Hirschel Grodzienski. "What's this all about, Hirschel?"

"They say Hitler is fleeing to Tyrol to keep up the war there. They need us to build a fortress for him to hide in."

Another man next to them scoffed. "That's another lie. The Nazis do not want to be caught with so many of us. Then the world will know what they have done. Did you not see the guards passing out food and clothing as we left? They are trying to smooth things over, to make the prisoners say how kind they were to us. The animals."

A third man whispered, "Kaltenbrunner will kill us all. Even in the death throes of the Third Reich, the Nazis will do their best to murder all the Jews."

And so they marched, rumors swirling up and down the line.

It was late at night in the former offices of the camp commandant. Gerd Hirschberg sat at a desk going over the lists of prisoners. He did not expect to find anything good about Emily's parents, but he looked anyway.

The record keepers divided the information in the records into five columns: family name or given name, place and date of birth, last place of residence, prisoner number and barracks, when they had arrived, and what had happened to them. Name followed name with "died" and the date in the last column. Gerd went through the files until he found the records from 1935 to 1936. Now he was going through them, name by name.

So many deaths ... This cannot be!

Gerd leafed through the records page by page until he came to March 1936. Then he saw the entry. There they were! Emilé and Rachel Weissbach from Munich. His eyes went to the last column. His heart sank. Rachel was dead—soon after they arrived, it appeared. He looked at Emilé's entry. The last column was empty! He checked again—there was no entry, it was blank.

This can only mean one thing. Emilé died within the last few days and the Germans did not have time to make an entry or ...

Gerd lifted the phone and called in his aide, Sergeant Rosko.

"Sir?"

"Sergeant, Have they dispersed the prisoners from the barracks yet?"

"No, sir. The transports to the hospitals have not arrived, so our men are making the survivors as comfortable as possible until they do."

"Good." He pointed to the map of the camp. "I want you to go to these barracks and find someone who has been in charge. Bring him to me."

"Yes, sir." Rosko turned and left.

In about half an hour, there was a knock on the door.

"Come." Gerd looked up.

Sergeant Rosko entered. He looked back. "Don't be afraid, come in. The captain only wants to ask you some questions."

Then a man shuffled through the door—or what was left of a man. Gerd shook his head in disbelief. The man before him was skin and bones, skeletal, but his eyes were alive.

Gerd motioned to the chair in front of his desk. "Sit, please," he said gently. The man complied.

"What is your name?"

The man lifted his head. "I am Yitzhak Perlman."

"Have you had some food? Blankets? Are you comfortable?"

"Yes, they fed us, Captain, but the food was too rich for my stomach. I threw up. The clean water was good, though."

Gerd turned to his sergeant. "Rosko, go down to the mess and have the cooks make some broth for these men. Something light that they can handle."

Rosko nodded and left.

Gerd looked at the man. "Mr. Perlman, was Emilé Weissbach in your barracks?"

Perlman nodded. "Until three days ago."

Gerd's heart sank. "He died?"

Perlman shook his head. "No, Captain. Before you got here, the Nazis rounded up several thousand prisoners and marched them out of camp. They went south. I think the Nazis were trying to get as many prisoners out of the camp as they could, so you would not see the enormous evil of what they have done here. I think they meant to kill us all, but you arrived too soon."

"And Emilé?"

"He was taken in the march. He was alive when last I saw him."

Alive! Emily's father is alive!

Gerd picked up the phone. The operator answered him. "Yes, put me through to the general's office immediately!"

ONE FOOT in front of the other. If I stop I will die.

The snow had started again and then stopped, but he did not feel the cold anymore. He had fallen into a rhythm with his feet—

Step, step, left, right, move or die, move or die ...

The men moved in a long column down the road. They had not rested for hours. The road wound through the trees, rising toward the mountains, and the man could see the tops of majestic peaks lifting over the horizon. Soon they came into an area of heavy woods where the trees grew right down to the road, muffling the sound of the marching feet.

Hirschel marched next to him. "Tyrol, they are taking us to Tyrol."

He answered his friend. "Does Hitler think he can hide in the mountains? His kingdom is over. Why doesn't he just let us go?"

Hirschel shook his head. "He is a madman. Even as his mighty Third Reich crumbles around him, he sits in Berlin like a horrible spider, spinning his webs and pursuing his murderous schemes. I think he will not rest until every one of us is dead, or he is dead."

Hirschel began to speak in a low monotone.

May the Lord answer you on the day of distress; may the Name of the God of Jacob fortify you.

May He send your help from the Sanctuary, and support you from Zion.

May He remember all your offerings and always accept favorably your sacrifices.

May He grant you your heart's desire and fulfill your every counsel.

As his friend spoke, the man began to speak the words with him...

We will rejoice in your deliverance and raise our banners in the name of our God; may the Lord fulfill all your wishes.

Now I know that the Lord has delivered His anointed one,

answering him from His holy heavens with the mighty saving power of His right hand.

Some rely upon chariots and some upon horses, but we rely upon and invoke the Name of the Lord our God.

They bend and fall, but we rise and stand firm.

Lord, deliver us; may the King answer us on the day we call.

The tears in his eyes surprised him...

TO SEEK AND TO FIND

The jeep rolled slowly down the snowy road. Ahead of him, Gerd could see the tracks of feet, hundreds of feet. All along the way, they had seen the bodies of dead men. He had stopped to look at the identification number tattooed on each arm. He had memorized Emilé's—123356. None of the men he saw were Emily's father.

Yeshua, help me!

They pushed on up the mountainous road. Above them, a Stinson Sentinel purred through the sky, looking for the column of prisoners. The snow thinned, and the grey curtain of clouds lifted. The radio in the back seat crackled to life. Gerd looked around. The radioman listened and then turned to Gerd. "Sir, the advance scouts have entered a village called *Waakirchen*, about a mile ahead. They found many dead and dying in the snow and a lot of prisoners wandering around but no Germans. The guards seem to have run away." Gerd pulled over and signaled the two platoons behind him. A young lieutenant raced to the side of the Jeep. He was Japanese, a member of the 552nd Division.

"Sir!"

"Lieutenant, get your men up the road on the double. Be sharp. It looks like the Germans have abandoned the prisoners, but there may be some up there still willing to die for the Führer. And once you have secured the village, have some of your men collect any dead bodies. We need to identify them for the record."

"Yes, sir." The young man shouted orders, and the two platoons of Japanese troops left on the run. Gerd shook his head.

Only in the American army could a German captain command a group of Japanese GIs ...

THEY HAD COME to a small village in the mountains. The guards let them rest in a large meadow. Then a German armored vehicle came roaring up. The man in the *Kübelwagon* shouted at the officer in charge. *"Die amerikanischen Truppen kommen!"*

The officer turned to his men. *"Töten Sie soviel Gefangene, wie Sie können!"*

Some guards began firing at the prisoners. Others threw down their guns and ran away.

Hirschel grabbed him. "Run, run for your life."

He ran toward the woods as fast as he could. Others were with him. He saw a man get shot, stumble, and fall. Then they were in the woods, racing through the trees ...

GERD PULLED INTO WAAKIRCHEN. In a large meadow outside of town, he found the 552nd boys rounding up the survivors. All around, there were mounds under the snow. He could see men lying on the ground, still moving. He called the lieutenant over. "Lieutenant, what's your name?"

"Ichiro Imamura, sir."

"Well, Lt. Imamura, I want your men to check every body in this meadow. Some of these prisoners are still alive."

"Yes, sir." The Lieutenant went off to gather his men.

Sergeant Rosko approached with an old man in a ragged coat and striped pants. "Sir, this man wishes to speak to you."

The old man spoke in German. "*Guten tag,*"

Gerd replied. "*Guten, tag, wie gehen sie?*"

The old man smiled. "Ah, you speak German? *Gut.*"

They continued speaking in German. Gerd asked the man what he needed.

"When the Germans started firing, many ran into the woods, maybe a few hundred. They are probably hiding, afraid of the Germans."

Gerd shook the man's hand. "*Danke*, now go with the soldiers, they will help you. We have trucks coming to take you back to the hospitals. We will find the others."

The old man bobbed his head and then shuffled away. Gerd turned to his Sergeant. "Rosko, get me twenty or thirty men. Bring them to me."

In a few minutes, Rosko was back with the men. Gerd addressed them. "There are several hundred prisoners hiding in those woods. We need to bring them out. As you walk through the woods, I want you to shout this phrase. '*Wir sind amerikanische Soldaten! Haben Sie Angst nicht. Sie sind jetzt sicher.*' It means 'we are American soldiers, do not be afraid, you are safe now.'"

Gerd led the men into the woods. They spread out—each shouting the phrase Gerd had taught them. Soon men came out from behind trees and out from under logs and brush. Soon there was a large group. Gerd stepped in front of them. "Emilé, Emilé Weissbach?"

A man stepped forward. "I am Hirschel, Emilé's friend. He fell back there. I think they shot him."

Dear Jesus, not after all this ...

"Show me!"

The man led, and Gerd and Rosko followed. They came to a small swale where a brook ran through the trees. "Emilé, Emilé Weissbach, can you hear me?"

Nothing. Gerd shouted again. There! A voice!

"*Ich bin hier...*"

Gerd pushed through the brush. A man in a ragged coat was lying beneath a tree. Hirschel ran forward and knelt down beside him. "Emilé, Emilé, are you hurt? I thought they shot you."

The man opened his eyes. He smiled. "*Nein*, Hirschel. These old legs just gave out, and I fell."

Gerd came and knelt beside Hirschel. "Are you Emilé Weissbach from Munich?"

"Yes?" A question came into the man's eyes.

"Do you have a daughter named Emily?"

Amazement came over Emilé's face. "Yes, I had a daughter, but she is dead. She must be dead."

Gerd laughed out loud. "Thank you, *Yeshua!*"

The two Jews looked at him in wonder. Gerd put his hand on Emilé's shoulder. "No, Emilé, she is not dead. She is safe in America."

"America, but how, when ...?"

"She is my wife, Emilé, I saved her from the Nazis when she came to my barn after they took you away."

"Emily, alive?"

"Yes, Emile, we live in Colorado, and now I will take you home to her. *Kumm.*"

Gerd put his arms under Emilé and lifted him. He was light as a feather. Gerd carried him through the woods and out into the meadow. There were jeeps and trucks waiting. Gerd laid Emilé on a stretcher. The soldiers lifted him into the back of a truck. Gerd climbed in after him. He turned to Rosko. "Sergeant, you work with Lieutenant Imamura and get the people on board and headed to the field hospitals. I'm going with my Papa."

Emilé looked up. "Papa?"

"Yes, Papa. You are coming to America with me. Emily is there. You will see her again."

Emilé's face twisted, and he wept.

And Gerd wept too.

WHO HAS BELIEVED?

*G*erd sat beside the bed of Emilé Weissbach in the field hospital and looked down at Emily's father. Though the face was haggard, worn, and pale, Gerd could see Emily there. Emilé had a drip solution of glucose attached to his arm. The curtain parted, and a doctor came in. "How's our patient doing?"

"He's sleeping, Doctor. What's the prognosis?"

"Well, apart from the fact that these despicable Nazis nearly starved him to death, he has a robust constitution, and I believe he will recover."

"Completely?"

"No, he will never be the man he once was, but with good care, he should be with you for quite a while."

"Yes, some of my *Mütti's Buttermilchsuppe* will be good for him." He smiled at the doctor. "Buttermilk soup with dumplings."

The doctor smiled back. "Sounds like just the ticket." He dropped the curtain and left.

Gerd turned back to Emilé. His eyes were open, and he was looking at Gerd. "So you found my little Emily in your barn?"

Gerd nodded. "Yes, she was hiding from the Nazis. She was

across the street from your house when the Nazis came. She saw everything. After they left, she took what she could and came to Saarbrücken, hoping to cross the border into France. But the German army had marched into the Rhineland, and she could not cross."

"So you kept her and fell in love with her?"

"From the first moment I saw her." Gerd felt himself blushing, and he lowered his head. "You have a granddaughter, Papa. Her name is Adina. Your friend, Joshua Rosen, named her."

"A granddaughter?"

"Yes, Papa."

Emilé turned away. Gerd heard him sob. "What is it?"

"No one has called me Papa since I last saw Emily and ... since ...."

"Since the SS killed Jürgen?"

"Yes, Gerd, since they killed my son."

Gerd put his hand on Emilé's shoulder. "Emily told me he was trying to defend you when the Nazis shot him."

Emilé nodded. "Yes, he was a wonderful son, strong and honorable."

"Well, the Lord has sent me to defend you now, Papa. I will do everything I can to get permission to bring you home with me. I lost my father many years ago, and now, I will be your son and take care of you."

"You said Joshua Rosen named my granddaughter. Where ... how ...?"

"We met him when the Nazis were sending us to Dachau on a train. They captured us. They said they were taking us to the camp, but on the way, the SS came and killed everyone on the train. Joshua saved us. He gave his life for us. It was through him Emily and I discovered that we have the same messiah, *Yeshua Hamaschiach*."

"Who?"

"The one you know as Jesus the Christ. He was your Messiah and mine too."

"But he was a Christian."

"No, Emilé, he was a Jew, a direct descendent of David on both sides of his family. The Torah speaks of him quite plainly."

"I have not read Torah for many years, but I do not remember that."

"Have you ever read Isaiah?"

"The prophet? Yes, of course."

"But you have not heard Isaiah 52:13 through 53:12?"

"I don't remember that."

"Because the Rabbis always skipped it."

"Why would they do that?"

"I'll show you."

Gerd reached into the pocket of his coat and pulled out a small Bible. He turned to Isaiah and read.

Behold, my servant shall deal prudently, he shall be exalted and extolled, and be very high. As many were astonished at thee; his visage was so marred more than any man, and his form more than the sons of men: So shall he sprinkle many nations; the kings shall shut their mouths at him: for that which had not been told them shall they see; and that which they had not heard shall they consider.

Who hath believed our report? And to whom is the arm of the LORD revealed? For he shall grow up before him as a tender plant, and as a root out of a dry ground: he hath no form nor comeliness; and when we shall see him, there is no beauty that we should desire him.

He is despised and rejected of men; a man of sorrows, and acquainted with grief: and we hid as it were our faces from him; he was despised, and we esteemed him not. Surely he hath borne our griefs, and carried our sorrows: yet we did esteem him stricken, smitten of God, and afflicted. But he was wounded for our transgressions, he was bruised for our iniquities: the chastisement of our peace was upon him; and with his stripes we are healed.

All we like sheep have gone astray; we have turned every one to his own way; and the LORD hath laid on him the iniquity of us all. He was oppressed, and he was afflicted, yet he opened not his mouth: he is brought as a lamb to the slaughter, and as a sheep before her shearers is dumb, so he openeth not his mouth. He was taken from prison and from judgment: and who shall declare his generation? For he was cut off out of the land of the living: for the transgression of my people was he stricken.

Gerd stopped and looked at Emilé. He was staring back at Gerd.

"Go on," he whispered.

And he made his grave with the wicked, and with the rich in his death; because he had done no violence, neither was any deceit in his mouth. Yet it pleased the LORD to bruise him; he hath put him to grief: when thou shalt make his soul an offering for sin, he shall see his seed, he shall prolong his days, and the pleasure of the LORD shall prosper in his hand. He shall see of the travail of his soul, and shall be satisfied: by his knowledge shall my righteous servant justify many; for he shall bear their iniquities.

Therefore will I divide him a portion with the great, and he shall divide the spoil with the strong; because he hath poured out his soul unto death: and he was numbered with the transgressors; and he bare the sin of many, and made intercession for the transgressors.

"But this is the suffering servant. This is the one foretold of in many parts of the Torah. The one who will come to save Israel."

"Yes, Emilé, and he came. To die on Passover as the perfect lamb for the sins of mankind, to rise from the dead after three days and nights as foretold in the Scripture, to send his Holy Spirit, the one he promised to the fathers by Jeremiah and Ezekiel, fifty days after he rose, on the day of first fruits, fulfilling all the Law of Moses."

"Can it be true?"

"Emilé, listen. I was a simple Amish farmer with a large farm. I was to be the elder of my community and live out my days in Ixheim, Germany. Then Emily appeared in my barn. We fell in love, married, then the Nazis captured us and sent us to Dachau. We escaped with the help of your Jewish friend, Joshua, which in Hebrew is Yeshua, and we came to America. Emily, and my mother and I became Americans. When war broke out in Europe, I joined the Army because they needed men who could speak German. They sent me back to Germany."

Emilé looked puzzled.

"Who else would save me, give me a wonderful wife and then bring me back to Europe and send me to find you in the woods? Who would keep you alive all those years so he could bring you back to life? And like he did for me, he did all these things to show you how much he loves you."

Emilé's eyes had tears in them. "Tell me more," he whispered.

And so the father back from the dead and the son who saved him began to speak of the wonder of the cross, until Emilé fell asleep in the wee hours of the morning.

Then Gerd kissed him on the forehead and arose and went to his bed, confident once more of the surety of his faith and the love of God.

THE DELAY—JULY 1945

*G*erd Hirschberg sat in the waiting room of the operations center of MI in the new Army Occupation Headquarters at Frankfort am Main. The building he was in had been part of the I.G. Farben complex during the war. Gerd found it fitting the military occupation of Germany centered in the building that had manufactured Zyklon B gas, the chemical used to exterminate so many Jews in the death camps.

A young WAC lieutenant appeared in the doorway. "Colonel Heym will see you now, Captain."

So Heym is a Colonel now. Good for him.

Gerd entered the office. Colonel Heym was sitting behind the desk, but he rose when Gerd came in. Gerd snapped a salute, but Heym came around, shut the door and shook his hand. "Never mind the formalities, Gerd. We're both Ritchie Boys, and it's good to see you. Haven't seen you since Dachau. Sit down and please be at ease."

Gerd sank into a chair.

He seems overeager to please. I wonder what's up?

After a few banalities about the weather and how everything

was going, Heym got to the point. "I've got your request for leave here on my desk. I'm afraid I can't grant it ..."

"But why?"

Heym held up his hand. "I can't grant it ... just yet. There is still some business I before I can send you home."

Gerd frowned. "But I need to get Emilé home to his daughter. Emily is not yet aware her father is alive, and I'm locked down. The brass won't let me send any messages home."

Colonel Heym picked up a folder from his desk. "And I'm afraid it's because of Mr. Weissbach that I can't send you home yet. Emilé Weissbach was on the front lines of the Communist movement, along with Werner Scholem and Joshua Rosen, during the 1930s. Now that we have defeated Germany, we have entered into a new struggle."

Gerd started to speak, but Heym held up a hand. "Our new struggle is with the Soviets."

"But they are our allies."

"Were our allies, Gerd. If we pull out of Europe, Russia will take over the whole shebang, and this continent will be one solid communist bloc from the Atlantic Ocean to Vladivostok. We have some German Communists who fled to Russia, but once they saw which way the wind was blowing, they slipped back into Germany before the Red Army and showed up on our doorstep."

"What's Emilé got to do with this?"

Heym cracked his knuckles, a habit Gerd found annoying, but he put up with it. "It seems Emilé knows these men, and I want him to be part of the interrogation, or at least be there to let the Commies know we are playing square with them."

Gerd shifted in his chair. "What do we need to find out?"

"As much about the Russian plans for Europe as possible. That's why I need you there. You are my best interpreter, and you have a way with the Germans that I don't have, since I'm Jewish and have a built-in hatred for Nazis."

Gerd grinned. "I'm not sure I am especially fond of them either."

"You know, Gerd, I am always amazed you seem to have lost your German accent. You speak English like a native. How did that happen?"

"When we got to Franc in 1937, there was a little enclave of American expatriates living in our village, and we got to know them well. I already spoke some English, but my long conversations with them helped me. Then when we bought land in Colorado, I met a bunch of sure-as-shooting cowboys who showed me the ropes with my horse business. When you work with those old boys, you can't hang on to any 'furriner' stuff. So I lost the accent as quickly as I could." Gerd smiled. "But it's still there a little."

"So about your leave..."

"All I want to know is when do I get to go home."

Heym stood up and went to the window. "I wonder how many barrels of Zyklon B the Germans made right here?"

"Colonel Heym, about my leave?"

Heym turned back to Gerd. "I'm authorized to make you a deal, Captain."

"A deal?"

"Look, Gerd, the American army is planning a big trial of the Nazis. It won't start until November. I need you here to do a lot of the prep work, and I need you to interrogate as many of the Germans, both communists and Nazis, as we can find. If you do that, not only will I give you leave, but I will expedite your honorable discharge from the Army, and you'll be home by Christmas."

"Christmas? But it's only July. I'm already due for discharge. The War is over, Colonel."

"Gerd, I know you should go home today, but I really need you."

"What about Emilé?"

"If you stay, I will promise Emilé will have his passport and visa and be free to go. If you don't, I can't guarantee anything."

Gerd stood up. "So you're blackmailing me, eh, Colonel?"

Colonel Heym shook his head. "Sit down, captain, have a smoke, relax please. Let me explain the situation." He came around the desk and offered Gerd a Camel.

Gerd took one, pulled out his Zippo and lit up. He took a drag and looked at his friend. "You know, Colonel, when I was Amish, I would never have smoked one of these." He took another drag. "I'm waiting, Colonel."

Heym lit a cigarette too and sat on the corner of his desk. "Emilé Weissbach was a big deal in the Communist party, pre-Hitler. Oh, he wasn't the spokesman or anything, but we know he was very close with Werner Scholem. Emilé Weissbach wrote a lot of the communist literature that got published under Sholem's byline in the Communist newsletter. Sholem got thrown in Dachau almost as soon as Hitler came to power. Weissbach went underground, but they got around to him, eventually."

"So?"

"We are still at war, Gerd, but not with the Germans."

"The Russians?"

"Yes. We allied with with Stalin to beat Hitler, but now we have to look at a new reality. The Russians are Communists. They want to make the entire world Communist. If America doesn't stand up to them, they will. Right now, the war with Germany is over. But the Japanese have not surrendered. What I tell you next is for your ears only and must never leave this room. Understood?"

Gerd nodded.

"We have a new secret weapon, a bomb of some sort. It's in the last stages of development, but the Joint Chiefs and President Truman are deciding whether to use it on Japan. They are certain it will terrify the Emperor into surrender. Once we deploy it, the Russians will do everything they can to get their hands on it. The

Soviets captured the Nazi V2 rocket facility and took a lot of the German rocket scientists prisoner. Now they can make long-range rockets, and they will want to put this new weapon on top of them. That would make them the world power. Lucky for us, we got some V2 rocket boys too, like Wernher von Braun and some of his buddies. So we have to find out as much about the Russian Communist internal operations as possible."

Gerd took another drag. "And that's where Emilé and I come in?"

Heym nodded. "Because of Emilé's relationship to these men, the government is very suspicious of him. They'd like to hold on to him. If it weren't for you, MI would be holding Emilé. But if he cooperates and does America a good turn, and seeing what great service you have rendered, I'm fairly sure I can get him to America."

"Fairly sure, Colonel?"

"As sure as I can be in these times. But it all hinges on you staying."

Gerd rubbed his chin. "Okay, let me talk to Emilé. I'll let you know first thing in the morning."

"Okay, Gerd, but remember—the deal means you stay until November."

"Understood, Colonel." Gerd rose to go.

"Oh, and, Gerd ..."

Gerd turned at the door. "Sir?"

"You're still under lockdown as far as communication goes. You can write one letter to your wife, but you cannot tell her when you will be home, nor can you tell her any of the details of your work. It will go through Army censors so watch what you say, understood? And no phone calls. We do not want your whereabouts known."

Gerd nodded. "Understood, Colonel. Understood."

A LIGHT IN THE DARKNESS—MONDAY, DECEMBER 17, 1945

*A*dina stood waiting while her mama placed the menorah on a small table in front of the window. Emily arranged it and then turned to Adina.

"Do you remember what comes first, Dina?"

"Yes, Mama. The blessing prayers to bless the menorah."

"How many, Dina?"

Adina thought for a moment. "Two ... no three, because tonight is the first night."

Emily smiled. "Yes, Dina, three prayers. Before lighting the menorah, we thank God for giving us this special mitzvah, and for the incredible Hanukkah miracles. I will say them."

She began. *"Baruch Atah Adonai Elohenu Memech haolam Asher kideshanu bemitzvotav vetzivanu lehadlik ner Chanukah."*

"Blessed are You, Lord our God, King of the universe who has sanctified us with His commandments, and commanded us to kindle the Hanukkah light."

Emily paused and then went on. *"Baruch Atah Adonai Elohenu Melech Haolam sheasa nisim laavotenu bayamim hahem bizman hazeh."*

"Blessed are You, Lord our God, King of the universe who

performed miracles for our forefathers in those days, at this time."

Dina tugged her mama's skirt. "Can I say the third one, Mama?"

Emily nodded. "Do you remember it, darling?"

"Yes, Mama, you wrote it down for me, and I memorized it."

Magda smiled at her precocious granddaughter. "Such a smart girl."

Emily nodded to her daughter. "Go ahead, Dina."

Dina took a deep breath. "*Baruch Atah Adonai Elohenu Melech Haolam shehecheyanu vekiyimanu vehigianu lizman hazeh.*"

"Blessed are You, Lord our God, King of the universe who has granted us life, sustained us, and, um ... oh yes... and enabled us to reach this occasion."

The two older women smiled at Dina. "Very good, Dina."

Emily took the candle that was standing in the cup in the middle of the menorah. "Now we will light the *Shamash.*"

She held the candle out, and Magda struck a match and lit it. She moved to the first cup on the right, which was filled with oil and had a wick floating in it. She lit the wick and then placed the *Shamash* candle back into its cup in the center. "We will leave the candles burning for one half an hour."

The light of the *Shamash* and the first candle flickered in the window, reflecting off the glass, a tiny light against the darkness outside. A gust of wind shook the glass as though the darkness wanted to reach in and snuff it out, but the candle and the lamp burned bravely, unbowed. Emily took Magda and Dina's hands in hers, and they stood silently watching the tiny flickering flames.

Dina spoke first. "Dear Jesus, please make this menorah be a light that will guide my papa home."

Dina felt her grandmother's hand squeeze hers. "Yes, Lord, please bring Gerd home to us safely through the storm."

AFTER ADINA HAD GONE to bed, Magda took Emily in the kitchen. "I was looking at the oil, and I don't think we have enough." She held up the bottle of olive oil. There was only a small amount in the bottom. "We have not been able to go to the store for a week. I thought we had more, but I looked everywhere and we do not."

Emily frowned. "But how will we light the menorah for eight nights? There is only enough here for three days."

"I don't know, Emily, I don't know. Unless we can get out to the store, I don't know how we will keep it lit for eight days. And I might not have enough flour to make *Stöllen*. Oh, I hope it stops snowing."

Emily patted Magda's hand. "Let's wait until morning, and we will see what happens. I think we just need to trust the Lord."

ACROSS THE PLAINS, huge dark clouds were massing as a cold front pushed into the San Luis Valley. The wind picked up, and the snow fell, thicker and faster. A rare blizzard was moving through from the mountains.

TUESDAY, December 18, 1945

In the morning, they looked out over a solid blanket of snow. At least three inches had fallen in the night, adding to the snow already on the ground. As Emily looked out the window, she saw an old Chevy truck making its way through the drifts on the road into their ranch. "Magda, Magda!"

Magda hurried into the room. "What is it, Emily?"

"It's Billy Roberts. He'll have news."

The truck pulled up in front of the house and Billy Roberts, a lanky man with a Stetson hat and a long handlebar mustache, climbed out. He trudged through the pristine snow to the front porch and knocked on the door. Emily flung it open. "Billy! Come in! Come in!"

"Morning, Emily, Magda!"

"Uncle Billy, Uncle Billy!"

Dina came rushing down the stairs and flung herself into the tall man's arms.

"Hey, hey, how's my little Buckaroo?"

"Just fine, Uncle Billy, just fine."

Billy turned to Magda. "Got any coffee for a poor old cowboy?"

Magda smiled and nodded and went off to the kitchen to fetch a cup.

Billy sat down at the dining room table. "Are you ladies all right? I tried to call, but the lines are down all over this part of the valley and Ma Bell can't get them fixed until after Christmas. I'd have come sooner, but I had to get the herd down into a closer pasture. I got them all down, including Gerd's, so we are good for the winter."

Emily gave Billy a hug. "Thank you, Billy, Gerd so appreciates that you've been watching the horses. And we do too."

"Well, no difference between taking care of a hundred and a hundred fifty. A lot of Gerd's mares are with foal, so come spring, your herd will increase."

Magda sat next to Billy. "Have you been into Alamosa?"

Billy pulled off his hat and laid it on the table. His long graying hair curled down around his collar. "Yeah, I went in for supplies, but the snow shut Highway 285 from Denver down and they have had no trucks in. They are expecting some just before Christmas."

"But that's a week away. I need flour and potatoes and ..."

"Oil," Magda said.

"Yes, oil."

"Cooking oil? I got some Crisco at the ranch."

"No, it has to be olive oil if I can get it."

Dina pointed to the menorah in the window. "For the Hanukkah lamp."

Billy shook his head and took a swig of coffee. "I don't know, Emily. Fred at the market is pulling his hair out. Christmas is coming, and people are running short on everything. I have extra flour and potatoes at my place, and I can bring some eggs and a side of ham over. I got plenty of beef in the freezer." He grinned. "I even have a turkey I can bring if I can stay and help you eat it. We won't starve before Christmas."

Emily smiled back. "You know you can. I was going to call and invite you, but ... no phone."

Dina piped up. "We have enough oil for the menorah, right, Mama?"

Emily hesitated and then looked at Magda. "I hope so, Dina, I hope so."

THE DOUGLAS DC-3 airliner droned on through the night. Captain Gerd Hirschberg sat in a seat next to the window, unable to sleep. Next to him, Emilé Weissbach snored. Gerd reached over and pulled the blanket up around the older man. The WAC flight attendant came down the aisle with some pillows. She saw that Gerd was awake and stopped. "Would you like a pillow, Captain?"

Gerd reached up and took one. "Thank you, Corporal. Maybe it will help me sleep."

The WAC corporal looked down at Emilé. "How's Mr. Weissbach doing? I don't see many civilians on military flights."

"He's fine. The Army took good care of Emilé after his liberation, and he's put on some weight. He earned his flight home by participating in some operations I'm not at liberty to speak about. I'm hoping to get him home by Christmas. His daughter, my wife, has not seen him since 1936. How much longer is the flight?"

"We'll be landing at Gander in about four hours. After that, we'll connect you with a flight to get you down to Presque Isle Army Air Field in Maine."

"Thank you, Corporal. You've been very kind."

The young woman smiled and headed back to her seat in the back of the plane. Gerd looked out the window. It was pitch black, with clouds hiding the stars. As he stared out, the clouds thinned and the plane came out into the open. Gerd gasped. The moon was full and shone down on the ocean, lighting the tops waves with millions of sparkling lights. Behind the moon the vast panoply of stars were set light diamonds in the vault of heaven. Gerd shook his head in wonder.

Once I was a simple Amish farmer in a tiny village in Germany. My future was before me, unchangeable. I would always be an Amish farmer, always live in Ixheim, grow old and die in Ixheim. Then you brought me Emily and now I am in an airplane flying over the Atlantic Ocean, flying home to America.

A verse from Romans came to him. "O the depth of the riches both of the wisdom and knowledge of God! How unsearchable are his judgments, and his ways past finding out!"

And then a voice in his heart he had not heard for a long time.

I am the light, Gerd. I will guide you home

IN HIS HANDS—FRIDAY, DECEMBER 21, 1945

*C*hicago's O'Hare Airport was crammed with holiday travelers and hundreds of servicemen. Gerd was speaking to a gum-chewing young lady who seemed more concerned about her makeup than getting him home on time.

"I'm sorry, sir, but we have delayed your flight to Denver. There is a big blizzard moving through, and they shut the airport." She looked at her schedules. "I'm sorry, nothing until Monday." Then she looked around and beckoned Gerd closer. "I'm not supposed to tell anyone because there are so many servicemen trying to get to Denver, but there are military flights going from here to the Army Airfield at Lincoln, Nebraska. If you go down those stairs and walk down the hallway, you'll come to the Army Air Force office. Maybe they can help you."

"Thank you, Miss." Gerd nodded to Emilé, and the two men headed for the stairs.

As they went down the stairs to the lower level, Emilé chuckled.

"What?" Gerd asked.

"I could have walked across Germany in the time we have

spent to get across your America. I did not understand it was so big."

"Wait until you see the San Luis Valley, Emilé. The mountains go to the sky, and the land has no limits. The horses run wild, and the farmers grow wonderful crops."

They walked down the hall and went into the office of the Army Air Force. A young sergeant was sitting at the desk. He stood and saluted.

"At ease, Sergeant. The war's over and I'm on my last duty—getting home for Christmas. I need a flight to Lincoln if I can get one."

"I'm sorry, Captain, but we do not book flights here—it's for equipment transport and getting our pilots to their duty stations."

"You mean you don't have a bare bench for a European vet and his father-in-law?"

"Well, I'm not sure, but if you gave me your name and the phone number where you are staying I could see if I can find something ..."

Gerd grinned. "Right now, we're staying in the airport lobby. So all you have to do is call us to the courtesy phone."

"I'll see what I can do—names, please."

"Captain Gerd Hirschberg and Emilé Weissbach."

The Sergeant looked up. "Did you say Weissbach?"

"Yes. Is something wrong?"

"No, I ... wait here a minute, Captain."

The sergeant got up and went through a door into an inner office. In a moment he returned with a major in tow. The sergeant pointed to Emilé.

The major came around the desk. "Is your last name Weissbach?"

"Yes," Emilé nodded.

"Well, this is a strange coincidence. I have never met another Weissbach before ... except for my family."

"Another?" Emilé said.

The major nodded. "Yes. My name is Edwin Weissbach."

Emilé stepped closer. "Are you Jewish?"

"Yes, I am."

"Where does your family come from?"

The major thought for a moment. "I believe from Munich. My grandfather came here right after World War I."

"And what was his name?"

"Awiezer Weissbach."

Gerd could see the astounded look on Emilé's face. "But this is not possible. My father had a cousin, Awiezer, who left Germany in 1922."

Now it was the major's turn to be amazed. "Yes! That's when grandfather came. So we are related? Distant cousins, it seems."

Gerd was smiling. *How do you do this, Lord?*

The major turned to Gerd. "Captain, what was your difficulty?"

Gerd shook his head in amazement. "We are trying to get to Denver, so we can get home to the San Luis Valley. This is Emilé Weissbach. He spent the last ten years in a Nazi prison camp. I am married to his daughter. We wanted to get home by Christmas. I was hoping to get at least as far as Lincoln and then go from there."

"Captain, have you men had breakfast?"

"No, sir."

Major Weissbach smiled. "Well, come with me. I'm buying. We have a couple of hours to kill, and I want to hear your story before you have to catch your plane."

"Our plane, Major?"

The major turned to the sergeant. "Get these two men seats on the C-47 that's headed for Lincoln at 11:00. And not the benches in the back. I want you to make sure they have backup crew seats."

The sergeant smiled. "Yes, sir. Right away, sir."

Major Weissbach turned to Emilé. "Come on, cousin. I want

to hear everything." He nodded at Gerd. "You too, Captain. I'm very interested in how you met your wife and how in God's world you found Emilé."

"Yes, sir."

Because it is God's world, major ... it is God's world.

IT WAS FRIDAY EVENING, but the sun was still pale in the leaden sky. Dina, Magda and Emily stood before the menorah. Emily picked up the bottle of oil.

"Shabbat starts at sundown today. It is forbidden to light a fire on Shabbat, so today we light the menorah before the Shabbat candles. We must leave the menorah lit for one-half hour after sundown. That means we have to add extra oil to the five lamps we are lighting. I'm not sure ..."

Dina smiled up at her mother. "Go ahead, Mama. There will be enough oil."

"How do you know that, Dina?"

"An angel told me."

Magda and Emily looked at Dina in amazement. Magda took Dina by the hand. "An angel, my Dina?"

"Well, it was in a dream, I think. I knew you and Mama were worried about the oil, and I was trying to find some more. I even prayed for it. Then in my dream, a man came, and he told me not to worry, there would be enough oil. So I believed him. I think he was an angel."

Emily slowly shook her head and poured the oil into the cups. "One... two... three... four..." She looked up. "And five, Dina. Your angel was right. But..." She held up the empty bottle.

"I think there will be more tomorrow, Mama."

Magda looked into Dina's eyes. "You know about the oil? How there is always enough each new morning?"

"No, *Mütti*, I did not know that. But in my dream, the angel was so real. He told me to have faith—that the menorah light would lead Papa home. So I have faith."

Magda looked at Emily. "And Jesus said, 'Verily I say unto you, Except ye be converted, and become as little children, ye shall not enter into the kingdom of heaven,'" she whispered.

Emily came over and took Dina in her arms. "We shall have faith then too, my daughter. Lord help our unbelief."

She stood and light the Shamash with a match. "Tonight is the fifth night of Hanukkah. *Baruch Atah Adonai Elohenu Memech haolam Asher kideshanu bemitzvotav vetzivanu lehadlik ner Chanukah ...*"

ALMOST CHRISTMAS—SATURDAY, DECEMBER 22, 1945

*G*erd and Emilé sat in a reception area in the Army Air Force Base at Lincoln, Nebraska, on Saturday evening. Christmas Eve was a day and a half away. Emilé put his hand over Gerd's. "It is fine, Gerd. We will get home at some point. You have tried very hard, but I think maybe our luck has run out."

They sat for several minutes. Finally, Emilé spoke again. "Why is Christmas so special to you? Is it the birth of this Jesus that you celebrate?"

Gerd nodded his head. "Yes, it is the time we welcome him into the world, but it's more than that, Emilé. In our house, we celebrate Christmas and Hanukkah together—a tradition we have. A unique one, I know."

"Christmas and Hanukkah together? That is interesting."

"It's because of the menorah that Emily brought with her from Munich."

"The menorah. Do you mean the golden lamp stand that my wife Rachel's father made?"

"The same one, yes."

"She saved it from the house?"

Gerd stretched his back against the hard bench and nodded. "Emily was across the street when they took you away. She saw everything, including the murder of Jürgen. After the Nazis left, she went in the house through the back door and took what she needed—money, her passport, a few clothes. Then she got on a train and headed west. She had to get off because she heard that the Nazis were blocking the roads. Emily walked for two days through the woods. She brought the menorah, because she knew it was precious, and she thought she might have to sell it to get to France."

Emilé nodded. "Emily was always resourceful. So you found her in your barn?"

"Yes, hiding under the hay mound. She was so beautiful and so brave. I loved her from the first moment I saw her."

Emilé looked away. "That is how I felt about her mother. The first moment I saw her, I knew Rachel was for me. We married, but then I followed Werner Scholem. Rachel, well she knew that communism was bad, a lie. But I was young and impassioned, and the words of Marx and Lenin sounded so fair, so real—to each as they need and from each as they can give. Everything shared. No more bosses or rulers. But it was a trap. The people at the top only wanted power for themselves. They did not care about the masses. Rachel knew this, but she was a good wife. She let me proceed in my foolishness."

Gerd nodded. "But she kept her faith in God?"

"Yes, and she taught Emily and Jürgen. I did not like it, but I let her do it. Then when they killed my son and took us away, it broke something in Rachel. She got sick and died soon after we arrived at the camp. I saw her on her last night. Before she passed, she told me that communism would not save the world, only *Gott* could do that. I did not want to hear it, but it was her dying wish for me to give it up. After that, I struggled with many questions, but after I had been in the camp for a long time, I heard about what Stalin was doing in Russia—murdering so

many who opposed him—then I saw that there was no difference between him and Hitler. They had different political views,
but they were after the same thing—absolute power over the
people. I think it was a joke that *Gott* played on me to steal the
best part of my life, my son, my wife ..." Emilé began to cry
softly.

"No, Emilé, *Gott* did not play a joke on you. There is someone
else who wanted to bring misery and death to you."

Emilé sniffled and wiped his eyes on his sleeve. "Oh, you
mean, *ha-Satan*, the Accuser?"

"That's the one. *Gott* has a better plan for you than Dachau.
Your Jewish prophet Jeremiah said 'For I know the thoughts I
think toward you, saith the LORD, thoughts of peace, and not of
evil, to give you an expected end.'"

"Jeremiah said that?"

"Yes, he did."

Emilé sat thinking for a minute. "So you said you have a
somewhat unique Christmas tradition because of the menorah?"

Gerd slowly nodded. "When she first showed it to me, Emily
set it on my kitchen table, and the sunlight came in the window
and refracted off the beautiful gold lamps. I believe that for the
first time in many years, the Lord himself spoke to me. He said, 'I
am the light.' I thought Emily said it, but now I'm sure it was the
Lord." He paused. "Then we discovered that Jew and Gentile
worship the same God, Jehovah, and share the same messiah,
Jesus. The menorah became a symbol to us of how God worked
through the Jews to bring salvation to the rest of us."

Emilé nodded his head slowly.

Gerd went on. "Then the other night, when we were flying
across the Atlantic, we flew out of the clouds, and the moonlight
lit the sea like diamonds—like a path heading west across the
ocean. And the Lord spoke to me again and reminded me. 'I am
the light, Gerd,' he said, 'and I will guide you home.'"

Emilé nodded and smiled. "And so it seems he has been

doing, but now we are stuck here and I do not think he has any more miracles for us..."

"Excuse me?"

The two men looked up. Standing in front of them was a young man in a suit of brown warehouse clothes. There was a patch on his chest that said FFE Transport.

"Excuse me, are you the two men looking for a ride to Denver?"

Gerd looked at Emilé and nodded. "Yes, we are."

"My brother Frank told me about you. He works here, and I bring frozen beef here from our warehouse in Denver. I'm deadheading back tonight, and I sure could use some company to help me stay awake. I got room in the front."

Emile laughed out loud. The young man looked puzzled. "What's funny?"

"*Hineni*, young man, *hineni*."

The comment puzzled the young man.

"It's a Hebrew word. It means 'here I am.' People in the Bible used to say it when God was about to test their faith."

Gerd spoke up. "We'll gladly accept your offer. We should get a thermos full of coffee and some dinner in us before we go. Then we'll have all night to tell you about faith—or the lack there of."

Both Gerd and Emilé burst out laughing.

The young man just shook his head. "Say, I'm not taking a couple of nut cases to Denver, am I?"

Gerd and Emilé laughed even harder. Gerd slapped him on the shoulder. "No, young man, no. We are perfectly sane, and I assure you, we can prove it."

They collected their things and followed the young man toward a dining area.

Gerd!

Gerd stopped and turned. Then he knew who it was. "*Hineni*, Lord, *hineni*."

SHABBAT HAD COME TO AN END. The sun had gone down, and it was time to light the menorah. Dina brought the bottle of oil to her mother. They all looked at it in wonder. The container was half-filled with oil.

Emily took the bottle. She poured the oil into the lamp cups. There was just enough for six cups. Emily prayed. "We thank you, oh King of the Universe, who maketh good things to spring forth from the earth."

She lit the Shamash. "Tonight is the sixth night of Hanukkah. *Baruch Atah Adonai Elohenu Melech Haolam sheasa nisim laavotenu bayamim hahem bizman hazeh ...*"

LATER IN THE small hours of the night, something awakened Dina. A sound? She got out of bed and crept to the door. Slowly, she opened it. The sound was coming from downstairs—music, a wind? She went down the stairs clinging to the railing drawn by ... There! Under the pantry door, a light! She slipped up to the door and opened it a crack. A man! A man in the pantry, the same man she had seen before. He was dressed in white and very tall, but somehow, she was not afraid. The light bulb hanging from the ceiling was not on, but light filled the room. The man turned.

"Hello, Adina."

"He... hello... again." Dina drew closer. "Are you an angel?"

The man smiled. "I am a messenger, yes. Don't be afraid. Your prayers and your faith have brought me. He wants me to remind you he is the light. The light will bring your Papa home. And he is bringing a very special Christmas gift."

The man reached out and touched the jar of olive oil. More light filled the room. "This miracle happened once before, a long time ago in Israel. I was there too." The man smiled and touched

Dina's face. "Go back to bed now, little one. Sweet dreams. Do not worry about your Papa. He is on his way."

When she awoke in the morning, Dina stretched beneath her covers. Hansli jumped up on the bed and bunted against her until Dina pulled her under to snuggle. "I had another wonderful dream last night, Hansli, such a wonderful dream."

A LIGHT FOR CHRISTMAS—MONDAY, DECEMBER 24, 1945

*G*erd and Emilé sat in a small diner just down the street from the Hertz Drive-Ur-Self building in Denver, Colorado. They had arrived in the city very early Sunday morning after the nine-hour drive from Lincoln. The young FFE Transportation man, Bert Hayes, had proven to be good company, and the three had talked most of the night, bolstered by a thermos of very strong coffee and some sandwiches they got from a lunch counter at the Lincoln Army Air Force base. Bert had dropped them at the Brown Palace Hotel in downtown Denver, where they got a room and grabbed some sleep.

Nothing was open on Sunday, so they stayed around the hotel. Gerd took Emilé to a movie in the afternoon—*Back to Bataan,* with John Wayne. Before the movie started, the Movietone newsreel came on with a story about the Nuremburg trials. When the camera showed Ernst Kaltenbrunner, Hermann Göring, and the rest of the Nazi criminals sitting on the bench, Emilé stiffened in his seat. Gerd heard him whisper, "Kaltenbrunner ..."

Then the newsreel cut to a story about the liberation of the death camps, and when Emile´ saw the pictures of the prisoners, he wept quietly. Gerd put his arm around the older man's shoulder and comforted him. When they left the theater, Emilé did not speak. He was pale and withdrawn. That night before they went to bed, Emilé turned to Gerd. "Thank you," was all he said.

On Monday morning, the hotel clerk told them where to find Hertz. They took a cab to the rental office. The Hertz rental man had rented all his cars to Christmas travelers, but there was a return coming in at 2:30 that afternoon. So now they were waiting.

"Did you try to call Emily?"

Gerd nodded. "All the phone lines in the valley are still down."

"So Emily still does not know about me?"

"No, Emilé. I think this will be the best Christmas surprise ever."

Emilé stirred his coffee. Gerd noticed Emilé put three teaspoons of sugar in before he drank it. He glanced at his watch. "It's 2:15, Emilé. We should go down to the rental place."

"Ah yes, Gerd, just let me finish this sweet concoction I have blended. Sugar was the thing I think I missed the most at mealtime in the camp. If you could call those meals." He smiled.

"Well, I don't think you'll miss it from now on, Papa."

At the Hertz office their car had come in early, so within a few minutes, they signed the paperwork and were ready to go.

The man at the desk pulled out a map. "They shut down highway 285 through Buena Vista, so you have to go the long way around by Pueblo. It adds fifty miles to the trip, so you'll get there after dark. Come on out back. And we'll get you into your car."

He took them into the lot and showed them a nice 1942 Oldsmobile. They put their things in the back and headed toward home.

EMILY STARED out the window just before sundown on Christmas Eve. The snow covered everything and stretched away to the horizon. A pale sun tried to break through the gathering clouds.

I thought he would be home by Christmas. Lord, where is Gerd?

BILLY HAD COME in the morning with a fresh-cut tree in the back of his truck, and they had set it up and spent some time decorating. The tree stood in a corner of the front room, draped with garlands, tinsel, and large golden balls. At the very top stood a beautiful angel.

Magda was in the kitchen making *stöllen* for Christmas Day. Billy had brought a large turkey with him, and it was hanging in the cold room waiting for morning.

Dina stood in front of the tree, looking up. She turned to her mother and pointed to the top of the tree. "That's my angel, Mama."

"Your angel, Dina?"

"Yes, the one I saw in the pantry. He was filling the oil bottle. At least I think he was ... it might have been a dream. But he was so real, and how else could the oil bottle get filled?"

"I don't know, Dina. I don't know."

AROUND FIVE O'CLOCK, they drove through Pueblo. Gerd stopped at a gas station and filled up the tank, and they grabbed some sandwiches at a local diner. The streets were gay with Christmas decorations and wonderful displays filled the storefront windows. People were out on the streets, and the mood was festive. Emilé looked around in amazement. "It will not be such a happy Christmas in Germany, I think."

At the gas station, the attendant, a gangly young man with a missing front tooth, checked their oil and water, cleaned the windows, and topped off the tank. "Which way you headed?"

"Alamosa. We're headed home for Christmas."

"You a vet?"

"Yes, my father-in-law and I just arrived from Europe."

"You fought against the Germans?"

Gerd smiled. "In my own way, son."

The young man put the cap back on the tank. "Gee, it must have been swell. I was too young to go. I was just going to sign up when the big show ended."

Emilé shook his head. "Not so swell, young man, not so swell."

"Well, take it easy. There's a big blow coming through down there, so drive safely."

JUST BEFORE SUNDOWN, the four people gathered by the menorah. The lights from the Christmas tree reflected off the wonderful golden lamp stand. As she filled all eight cups, Magda told Billy about the oil that had not run out.

"Well, don't that beat all," he shook his head and smiled. "Christmas is a time for miracles, I guess."

Dina took his hand and held it. "And Hanukkah too, Uncle Billy, Hanukkah, too."

Billy looked down at Dina. "Yep. Hanukkah too, Buckaroo."

Emily lit the Shamash. "Today is the final night of Hanukkah. In our house, this is also the night before the day we celebrate the birth of Yeshua Hamashiach, Jesus Christ the Messiah. On this night, the Jews stood in the temple and gazed in wonder at the lamps that remained lit for five more days than they expected. Not too long after that, all the angels in heaven celebrated the birth of the Son of God. So we too celebrate the menorah that has remained lit five days longer than we expected, and we join all the angels in heaven as we say, 'Joy to the World, the Lord has come. He is the light of this world. Whoever follows him will not walk in darkness but have everlasting life ...'"

Dina bowed her head. "Dear Jesus, please bring my papa home to us safely." She looked up at Emily. Her mama was wiping the tears away from her eyes and nodding. "Yes, Lord, please ... *Baruch Atah Adonai Elohenu Memech haolam Asher kideshanu bemitzvotav vetzivanu lehadlik ner Chanukah ...*"

THE OLDSMOBILE CHUGGED through the darkness. The wind had whipped up, and snow was blowing across the road, making it very difficult to see. Gerd and Emilé had passed through Alamosa and were on the last twenty mile stretch to the ranch. Gerd was driving slowly.

"It is very hard to see the road, Gerd?" Emilé asked.

"Yes, Papa, very hard."

Just then something came at them out of the darkness—a large black shape. "A cow!" Gerd shouted and jerked the wheel. The car spun slowly to the right and powered off the edge of the road into the ditch. They came up against the bank with a shock, and then the engine died.

Gerd reached for Emilé, who had fallen against the passenger door. "Emilé, Emilé, are you all right?"

Emile sat up slowly, rubbing his head. He smiled, but his face was pale in the light from the headlamps. "Yes, Gerd. Aside from the fright and a minor bump on the head, I am still alive."

Gerd got out of the car. The headlights angled out over the fields and the wind caught at his coat. He walked around the car and then got back in. He tried to start the car, but it just made a grinding sound and then quit. Gerd shook his head. "I'm afraid we are stuck here."

THE MENORAH HAD BEEN BURNING for a half hour after sundown. It was time to extinguish the candles. Emily sighed and reached over to snuff out the first wick.

"Wait, Mama!" Dina clutched at Emily's arm. "Don't put them out yet!"

"But Dina, the oil is almost gone."

"Don't put them out yet, Mama. The light is bringing Papa home."

Emily looked down at her daughter's eager face. Then she looked over at Magda. Magda shrugged. "What can it hurt, Emily? Let them burn until the oil runs out."

And so the light from the menorah candles kept burning in the window.

THE HOMECOMING

*T*he inside of the car was growing bitterly cold. Emilé spoke in the darkness. "Can't we walk to the ranch, Gerd?"

"If I could see the way, if it was daylight, yes. But the snow has covered everything. I would not know which way to go. I'm sorry, Emilé. To have come so far and now this ..."

Just then, Emilé put his hand on Gerd's arm. "What is that sound?"

Gerd listened. At first he heard nothing and then, faintly, tinkling in the darkness ... "Bells? It sounds like jingling bells, Emilé. What in the world ..." They both stared out the window.

Out of the darkness, a large black shape loomed up. A horse! And then behind the animal appeared a sleigh with the figure of a man sitting wrapped in a heavy blanket. A white bushy beard poked out above the collar of his coat. Sleigh bells covered the harness and they jingled softly in the wind.

Emilé rubbed his eyes. "The cold has addled my brain. I'm seeing *Weihnachtsmann*."

Gerd shouted. "No Emilé, it's not Father Christmas. It's Jakob

Shrock!" He turned to Emilé. "It is one of my Amish neighbors. He is driving his sleigh. Thank you, Lord!"

Gerd jumped out of the car. "Jakob! Jakob Shrock! It's me."

The old man in the sleigh pulled the reins, and the horse stopped next to the car. "Who is it? Do you need help?"

Gerd shouted against the wind. "It's me, Jakob! Gerd Hirschberg. We are stuck in the ditch."

The old man stared down at Gerd. "Gerd! Gerd Hirschberg, you are home at last. *Kumm!* Get in the sleigh. I will take you to your house."

"But the snow, Jakob, how will you see?"

Jakob laughed. "I don't need to see. Freyla will take us home. Her dinner is in my barn. The road to my barn runs right past your gate. Get in! Get in before you freeze to death."

Gerd helped Emilé out of the car and they clambered into the back of the sleigh. Jakob shook the reins, and they set off into the darkness.

———

Two hours after sundown and the menorah continued to burn, its bright steady light reaching out into the storm.

———

The wind howled around them, but Gerd and Emilé were warm under a huge robe in the back of the sleigh. "It's a buffalo robe, Emilé. It's from a bison. They used to roam this country by the millions."

Jakob turned and shouted back. "We are close, but I can't see anything. Freyla will just keep going unless I can find the gate."

And then, like a searchlight, a brilliant light flashed across the road ahead of them.

Jakob shouted. "There! I see your house. There is a light! I see it."

Gerd and Emilé stared at the light. It flooded the snow with glory, and Gerd could see the window of his house down the long driveway. In the window he could see something golden.

"The menorah, Emilé! They have lit the menorah for Hanukkah, and it is guiding us home."

Jakob laughed and chucked the reins. Freyla turned into the road to the house and they headed toward the light.

DINA HEARD THEM FIRST. "Bells, Mama, I hear bells, sleigh bells!"

Magda, Emily, and Billy turned toward the window. Yes! Bells.

Dina ran to the door. There were heavy steps on the porch and a knock. Dina pulled the door open. Standing there was an old man with a white beard—their Amish neighbor, Jakob.

Emily went to the door. "Jakob Shrock, what are you doing out in this weather?"

Jakob laughed. "I was coming back to my house, and I found someone on the road. I have brought them home."

He stepped aside and there was Gerd, smiling and covered with snow.

"Papa!" Dina cried. She flew to Gerd, who picked her up and held her close. Emily and Magda just stared at him. Then Emily shrieked. "Gerd! Gerd!"

Gerd put down Dina and opened his arms. Emily came into them. "Gerd, you are home, you are home." She began to cry as she clung to him. Dina gripped his legs. Magda came and Gerd put one arm around her. "Hello, *Mütti,* I am home."

The four of them stayed that way for a long time. Then Emily noticed someone was standing behind Gerd. She wiped her eyes. "Who have you brought with you, Gerd?" She brushed more tears from her eyes.

"Hello, Emily." Emilé smiled.

Emily took a step closer. "Who are you?" Then she opened her eye wide. "Oh *mein Gott!*" She closed and then opened her mouth. "But, but ... you are dead!"

"No, daughter, I am very much alive, thanks to Gerd ... and your Jesus."

"Papa?" She took a step closer and touched Emilé's face. "Papa, is it you?" Then Emily was in his arms and clinging to Emilé and sobbing, and Emilé was weeping. And everyone was weeping and then laughing and the joy of Christmas filled the house.

Then the last of the oil ran out and the menorah candles went out, one by one.

AND SO THAT is the story of the Christmas miracle. So long ago, but I remember it so clearly. *Grossdáddi* Emilé came back from the dead to live with us for the rest of his life. My papa was back from the war, and my mama and my *Mütti* were happy again. My papa raised Mustang horses, and one day, I had a little brother, Jürgen, and our house was always full of light and laughter. Every year, we lit the menorah in the window. And we never forgot how the Light of the World brought my papa home.

Adina Hirschberg Thompson

Chapter Six

DECISIONS

... *E*very year we lit the menorah in the window. And we never forgot how the Light of the World brought my papa home.

Adina Hirschberg Thompson

ABIGAIL SAT QUIETLY for a long time after Uncle Jürgen read the last words of the story and closed the binder. Finally, she spoke.

"Wonderful, Uncle Jürgen, simply wonderful. What a beautiful story!"

Jürgen nodded, a smile on his lips. "*Ja*, my sister, she could tell a story. I miss her. It was a sad day when she left Alamosa with Peter Thompson."

"What happened, Uncle Jürgen?"

"Peter Thompson was an *Englischer*, a fellow who was not Amish. He was the son of a local rancher. He and Adina knew each other from growing up, but something deeper happened between them when they went to college together. She was taking a writing course, and he was studying to be an engineer."

"Was that a bad thing, that he was not Amish?"

"Well, that's a good question, Abigail. My *daed* was what you might call semi-Amish. He had a real go-round with the Amish church back in Ixheim, Germany, when he married Emily, my mother. They kicked him out of the church, and it was an Amish woman who wanted to marry him who turned Emily and Gerd in to the Nazis. So, by the time he got to Colorado, he settled on just being a westerner who raised horses, and leaving his old life behind. But my grandmother got very involved with the local Amish community, who had a different slant on things than the folks in Germany, so *Daed* never really got away from his Amish roots."

"So, it's wrong for Amish to marry outsiders? I mean..."

"The Amish pretty much try to stay within their own group when it comes to marriage."

"So, was there trouble when Adina fell in love with Peter?"

"First, my *daed* didn't see eye-to-eye with Peter's father. There had always been a kind of friendly competition between them as to who could raise the best horses. But something happened in a horse trade, and Pop felt that Gordon Thompson had cheated him. So, he wasn't keen on Peter and Adina's romance. And even though he tried to be more open-minded, he really couldn't leave his Amish life behind. So, he didn't give his blessing."

"And that hurt Adina?"

Jürgen nodded. "Very much. We have always been a tight family, and Adina couldn't understand why he wouldn't want her to be happy, while my *daed* thought he was doing what was best for his daughter."

"What happened?"

"Peter got his degree in engineering and got offered a very lucrative job in Alaska, working for an oil company. He and Adina eloped and left the valley. Adina wasn't baptized in the Amish Church, so she didn't go under the shunning, but my pop still pulled back from their relationship. He felt she had gone against his wishes, and she thought he should support her in her life choice. So, she left. It was a very painful time. I don't think my parents ever got over it."

"So, when she wrote these stories, she was married to Peter and living in Alaska?"

Jürgen nodded. "Yes. I think she wanted to heal the breach, so she wrote the stories and sent them to my *daed*. I think it helped, but before they could really reconcile, Adina got sick and died." Jürgen looked away. "A very sad time."

Abigail moved over on the couch next to Jürgen. He put his arm around her. "Thank you for sharing that story, Uncle Jürgen. So..." she hesitated. "Adina really saw an angel?"

Jürgen smiled. "Yes, she swears she did, and the angel came each night and filled the bottle of oil in the pantry with enough to keep the menorah burning the next day. It was the miracle of Hanukkah and the miracle of Christmas rolled into one."

"And I thought angels were just in books." She sighed. "I have a lot to think about."

THAT NIGHT SOMETHING woke Abigail out of a troubled sleep... a sound... the wind, maybe. She turned over in the bed and saw a light coming in under her door.

Uncle Jürgen must be up...

She got out of bed and went to the door. As she opened it, a soft light flooded the room. There was a man standing in the hallway. He was dressed in white and very tall, but somehow Abigail was not afraid. He looked at her and smiled.

"Hello, Abigail."

Abigail stared. Finally, she spoke. "Are you Adina's angel?"

"I am a messenger, yes. And yes, Adina is my friend. But I have not been here for many years. Not since your uncle stopped lighting the menorah."

"He stopped?"

"When Adina left, she took Jürgen's joy. You must help him. Tomorrow is *Yom Rishon shel Hanukkah,* the first day of Hanukkah. And Abigail..."

"Yes?"

"Christmas is coming."

The light faded.

IT WAS MORNING. Abigail awoke. As she lay in the warm bed, she remembered.

It must have been a dream... And yet...

She dressed quickly and went down to breakfast. Her uncle was bustling about the kitchen. There was a stack of pancakes on a plate and some eggs and bacon in the pan.

"Good morning, girl."

"Uncle Jürgen, today is *Yom Rishon shel Hanukkah.*"

Jürgen looked at her with utter amazement on his face. "How in the world did you know that?"

"Adina's angel told me."

Jürgen's mouth opened, and he stared at his niece. "He was here?"

"I think so. I was thinking it must have been a dream. But he said he had not visited since you stopped lighting the menorah."

Jürgen sat down on a chair abruptly. He stared at the floor for a long time. "He's right, you know. My mom kept lighting it after Adina left, but for me, the joy was gone. When my folks passed, I just couldn't do it anymore." He put his hand over his eyes. "I miss Adina. She was a light in my life. Always there for me." He wiped his eyes.

Abigail sat down next to her uncle and put her hand on his arm. "I don't know the first thing about Hanukkah or the menorah, but I think this year it's important... for you and for me. Can we light it?"

Jürgen looked up and nodded. "Maybe you're right. Maybe we need it." He stood. "We'll light it after dinner." He took a deep breath. "Now we're burnin' daylight, so we better get at these hotcakes while they're still hot. We got horses to feed."

THAT EVENING after they cleared the dishes, Jürgen went to his room. When he came back, he had a wooden box. He opened it and took out something wrapped in a dark cloth. He laid it on the kitchen table and unwrapped it, then stood it up. Abigail gasped. It was beautiful, golden. It gleamed in the light. It was like a candlestick, but it had eight branches, each with a cup on the end, and a ninth branch in the center.

"This is the *menorat Hanukkah*, the menorah my mother brought with her from Germany. It is solid gold, made by my great-great-grandfather in Poland. Most menorahs only have seven branches, but since this commemorates the eight days of Hanukkah, it has eight branches and the ninth for the candle to light the wicks. I haven't had it out for twenty years." Jürgen nodded for Abigail to follow. They went into the front room with the menorah and the box. There was a small table set in front of the window. "Usually, a Jewish household will place the menorah on the mantel. But 'round here we have a different tradition."

He placed the menorah on the table in front of the window. There was a small bottle of oil in the box, and Jürgen used it to carefully fill the cups. Then he took some small wicks out of the box and floated them in the oil. He took a regular candle and placed it in the cup at the center of the menorah. "This is the *shamash*, the servant candle. We use it to light the other eight wicks during the eight days of Hanukkah. Before we light it, we will say three prayers because it is the first night, and on this night, we thank God for giving us this *mitzvah*, a religious commandment to celebrate the Hanukkah miracles." He took Abigail's hand and prayed.

"*Baruch Atah Adonai Elohenu Memech haolam Asher kideshanu bemitzvotav vetzivanu lehadlik ner Chanukah.* Blessed are You, Lord our God, King of the universe, who has sanctified us with His commandments, and commanded us to kindle the Hanukkah light."

He paused, and then continued. "*Baruch Atah Adonai Elohenu Melech Haolam sheasa nisim laavotenu bayamim hahem bizman hazeh.* Blessed are You, Lord our God, King of the universe, who performed miracles for our forefathers in those days, at this time."

Jürgen paused and reached into his pocket. He handed Abigail a piece of paper. "I'll say the Hebrew and then you read this." He began. "*Baruch Atah Adonai Elohenu Melech Haolam shehecheyanu vekiyimanu vehigianu lizman hazeh.*"

Abigail looked at the paper and read it. "Blessed are You, Lord our God, King of the universe, who has granted us life, sustained us, and enabled us to reach this occasion."

Then Jürgen reached into his pocket and pulled out a wooden match. He scratched it across the stone face of the fireplace and then lit the *shamash.* He lifted the wax candle and moved to the first cup on the right to light the wick. A soft glow of light reflected off the window glass. Jürgen smiled. "It's good; I'd forgotten how much it meant to us. We will let it burn for half an hour."

Abigail watched the candles flicker. She slipped her hand into her uncle's and they stood quietly.

Jürgen spoke. "Hanukkah means dedication. At Hanukkah, we celebrate the restoration of the Temple in Jerusalem that a profane Gentile king made unusable for the Jews. *Daed*, with his experiences in Germany and then when he found his father-in-law at the end of the war, always told us kids what Hanukkah meant to him. He spoke to us while the candles burned."

"Tell me, Uncle Jürgen."

Jürgen led Abigail to the couch. "Here's what he told us, and it stuck with me all my life. First, never be afraid to stand up for what's right. The Jews who won their revolt stood up against great odds. My *daed* stood up against his own church and against the Nazis and rescued my mother and her father from certain death. Second, he told us always to increase in doing good in the world. He used the example of each candle adding more light to the room over the days of the celebration to picture it. We need to be a light in the world. And he always told us that a little light goes a long way. When he and my grandfather Emilé lost their way in the storm, the light of one candle in the window would not have been enough to guide them home. But my *maam* kept all the candles burning, and the angel used them together to make a glorious light that cut through the darkness. And my father was never ashamed of his faith in the Messiah. So, I have to thank you, Abigail."

"What for, Uncle?"

"Jesus told us we should be a light on a hill. But I've been hiding my light under a basket. I've been out here on this ranch like an old hermit. We had the best of both faiths in our home, the Jewish roots, and the fulfillment of all that in our relationship with Jesus. I'd forgotten, and now, I believe God has sent you to me to help me remember."

"Do you really believe that, Uncle Jürgen? Could God love me? I'm not a good person. I've done bad things and believed foolishly. Doesn't that disqualify me?"

"Jesus meets each of us and leads us to faith when we are still sinners. I don't earn salvation because I'm a good person; God gives it to me freely. Romans chapter five, verse eight says, 'God demonstrates His own love for us in this: While we were still sinners, Christ died for us.'"

"Did He die for me too, Uncle Jürgen? It's hard for me to wrap my mind around."

"Well, let's talk about it more each night after we light the candles."

"That would be wonderful. Oh, and, Uncle Jürgen... the angel told me one more thing."

"What's that?"

"He said, 'Abigail. Christmas is coming.'"

Chapter Seven

A CHRISTMAS BLESSING

*A*nd so, each night for the next seven nights, they lit the menorah and prayed the two blessings. Abigail learned them and soon she was praying the Hebrew with Jürgen.

Baruch atah, Adonai Eloheinu, Melech haolam, asher kid'shanu b'mitzvotav v'tsivanu l'hadlik ner shel Hanukkah.

...Followed by *Baruch atah, Adonai Eloheinu, Melech haolam, she-asah nisim la'avoteinu bayamim hahem bazman hazeh.*

Two days before Christmas, Jürgen came into the house at daybreak. Abigail was making breakfast.

"*Kumm,*" Jürgen said, pointing to the door. "Help me bring in the *Weihnachtsbaum.*"

"Weihnachtsbaum?"

Jürgen grinned. "The Christmas tree. Can't have Christmas without a tree."

Abigail went out with Jürgen. Just outside the back door was a beautiful silver spruce, lying in the snow. Jürgen stood it up. "I have a stand in the shed. We'll take the tree in, and I'll fetch it."

They carried the tree into the front room. Jürgen pointed to the corner of the room across from the fireplace. He chuckled. "We always set it in that corner so we wouldn't burn the house down. Wait a minute." He went out and returned with a sturdy metal stand. He fastened it to the base of the tree, and they stood it up in the corner. The stand had a bowl which Jürgen filled with water.

"Keeps it fresh."

The tree was lovely but bare.

"What about decorations?"

"Decorations we got. Come with me to the attic."

They went down the hall and up the stairs to the second floor. At the end of the upstairs hallway was a pull-down trapdoor. Jürgen pulled the rope, and a set of stairs leading to the attic unfolded neatly.

"I haven't been up here for twenty years. But all my *maam's* Christmas stuff is up here. A real treasure trove."

They went up the stairs and, at the top, Jürgen pulled a string that was dangling down in the dark. A single bare bulb hanging from the center of the ceiling rafter clicked on, lighting up the corners of the dusty attic. Bare boards and studs lined the walls. A few cobwebs reflected the light. Against one wall was a stack of boxes with 'Christmas' written on them. Jürgen went over and pulled out three or four. He handed one to Abigail. "We'll come back for these others. Watch your step going down."

They each carried a box to the front room. Abigail opened them, marveling at the beautiful decorations. "Bubble lights, Uncle Jürgen! I haven't seen those in years."

"Hope they still work."

Soon the tree was ablaze with light and ornaments. Jürgen looked at Abigail and put his hand on her shoulder. "Thank you, girl. I haven't celebrated Christmas since my folks passed. You've brought life back into the old place."

Just then, there was a knock on the door. Abigail went.

Maggie and Johan were standing on the steps with baskets in their hands. Maggie smiled and handed her basket to Abigail.

"Merry Christmas. Brought a few treats since I know that old coot can't even make a good cup of coffee."

Abigail carried the basket into the dining room and set it on the table. She began taking out the goodies. There was raspberry jam, caramel-covered popcorn, cookies filled with fruits and nuts, and a large loaf of what looked like bread dusted all over with powdered sugar.

Jürgen looked at Maggie with a huge grin. "Why you! You made *stöllen!*"

"Well, don't eat it all—share some with the girl."

Abigail looked over at Johan, who was standing quietly. He lifted his basket. "I have something for you, Abigail. I'm bringing it early. You might find a use for it."

He uncovered his basket and brought out a set of beautiful hand-carved wooden utensils—a deep spoon, a two-pronged fork, and a spatula—and gave them to Abigail. "Merry Christmas."

Abigail thought she had never seen anything so lovely. The handles had a wonderful spiral design with a small flower on the end, and the wood was dark. She looked up at Johan. "These are perfectly lovely, Johan. You made these?"

Johan nodded.

Maggie smiled. "He's been working on them since you got here."

"Thank you so much, Johan. I love them." She started to give him a kiss on the cheek, saw his blush and thought better of it. "I have something for you, too. I was going to wait until Christmas, but now seems like a good time. Be right back."

In a moment she returned with a small wrapped package. She handed it to Johan. "It's not nearly as artistic as what you gave me, but I wanted to give you something useful. I hope you like them."

Johan took the package and opened it. Inside were a pair of

top-grain leather, lined winter work gloves. Johan smiled and tried them on. He held up his hands to show everyone. "Timing is everything, Abigail. I just wore my last pair out. Thank you; it's very kind of you."

Now Abigail was blushing.

Jürgen stepped in to save the moment. "Well, let's make some coffee and have some of this stöllen. We can sit in the front room and admire the tree."

Maggie started for the kitchen. "I'll make the coffee. And you know we are inviting you to 'Second Christmas,' Abigail." She nodded at Jürgen. "And you can bring him if you can get him out of bed."

Abigail looked at Johan. "What's Second Christmas?"

Johan smiled. "Because Christmas is so important to the Amish community, it is celebrated for two days. On December 25, we meditate and read scripture at home. December 26, or 'Second Christmas,' is the day we celebrate with family and friends with festive gatherings. We have sumptuous feasts and exchange practical gifts. My favorite day of the year."

"It sounds wonderful."

While Maggie and Jürgen got the treats together, Johan pulled Abigail aside. "I have something I need to ask you."

They went out into the hallway.

"What, Johan?"

He looked at her and then came straight out. "Abigail, I have never met a more beautiful girl than you. You are beautiful inside and out. I... well, I have feelings for you, and I want to ask you if I can court you."

"Court me?"

"Yes, usually it's when an Amish man asks permission of the girl's parents to visit her more formally with the intention that somewhere down the road, they will be married. I don't exactly know who to ask so I'm coming to you directly."

Abigail's eyes opened wide, and she put her hand over her

mouth. She stared at Johan. Then she took his hand. "I am very honored, Johan, and I must admit I have feelings for you, as well. But I am not Amish. And, from hearing what happened with Adina, I know that it can be difficult if both parties aren't of the Amish faith."

He smiled at her. "Well, you are almost Amish. If you married me, we could fix that easily."

She took his hand. "You are a wonderful man, Johan, but the truth is... I haven't even worked out my relationship with Jesus yet, although, after talking with Uncle Jürgen, I am beginning to understand what that means. And I'm thinking about going back to school. So, because of all that, I know I'm not ready for the kind of commitment you want." She looked up at him. "Will you please give me some time to sort things out before I say anything in response to your request? I need to make some decisions about what I want to do with my life first. In the meantime, I am very happy to be your friend."

Johan looked away and then back. "I will do whatever you ask."

"Thank you, Johan." And then she did reach up and kiss him on the cheek.

ON THE LAST night of candle lighting, which was also Christmas Eve, Jürgen and Abigail lit all eight candles just after sundown. They sat in the front room in front of the fire watching the beautiful light from the menorah.

Jürgen reached into his pocket and brought out an envelope. "My family used to give gifts on Christmas Eve, so I have this for you." He handed it to Abigail. She took it and opened it. Inside the envelope was a single key.

"What's this, Uncle Jürgen?"

"It's the key to my house, but even more, it is the key to my heart." He turned on the couch and faced her. "I want to ask you something, Abigail. Ever since you came, even though we didn't get off to a great start, this old place has come alive. You have brought something sweet and lovely here with you, and it has changed me. I never married and have no children, and I had set myself to just getting old and disappearing. Now that you are here, I feel like I have a family again. So, I'm asking you to stay. Since your folks are gone, I want you to be like my daughter, live here and give an old man some light in my last days. Will you?"

Abigail stared at Jürgen and then put her hands over her face and burst into sobs.

"What is it, girl? Did I say something wrong?"

Abigail shook her head and looked up, tears running down her face. "No, Uncle Jürgen, you just said the most wonderful words I have ever heard. I... I love it here, and I've grown to love you, too. You have been so kind to me. I could not ask for a better Christmas gift than to stay here with you. Thank you! Oh, thank you!" She put her head down on Jürgen's shoulder and cried again.

"There, there, girl. I should be the one crying. By saying yes, you have blessed an old man more than you will ever know." He reached into the drawer of the coffee table and pulled out the tissues, took some, and handed them to Abigail.

She wiped her tears. After a few minutes, she looked up. "I have one more question, Uncle Jürgen."

"What's that?"

Abigail took a deep breath. "Do you think God... I mean, do you think Jesus... could they actually accept me with all my faults and all my mistakes?"

Jürgen pulled Abigail under his arm. "The mercy and grace of the Lord Jesus Christ extend to the highest of heavens and the lowest of the low. For God so loved the world, He gave His only begotten Son, that whosoever... and that's the important part... whosoever believes on Him will receive eternal life. When He rose out of Joseph's tomb, He brought a new creation with Him, a creation that is free from sin and guilt and every mistake. And all we have to do to become part of that creation is to believe that God gave Jesus as the only remedy for our broken condition."

"And if I believe, I can have that?"

"Absolutely."

"Then, that's what I want for Christmas, more than anything. You have shown me what true love can be, and I know it's because you love God… What do I have to do?"

Jürgen took her hands. "We've talked about this, and now I'm going to ask you three questions. First, do you believe Jesus died for your sins, all of them?"

Abigail nodded. "Yes, I do."

"And do you believe he was in the grave for three days and three nights and then rose again from the dead?"

"Yes, I do."

"And last, do you believe many witnesses saw him alive, and He is alive today to make you a new creation in Him? And that He is Lord?"

"With all my heart."

"The Bible says, 'If you declare with your mouth, Jesus is Lord, and believe in your heart that God raised him from the dead, you will be saved.' So welcome to the family. To God's family and to our family. You have just received the greatest Christmas blessing anyone could receive. A new life."

Abigail looked around at her new home. "I believe that, Uncle Jürgen. Thank you."

Jürgen held her close and kissed her on the forehead.

And as they watched, the candles on the Amish menorah flickered and went out one by one. Christmas came a few hours early that night.

EPILOGUE

Abigail

a nd that's the story of how I came home—home to my Amish
roots and to my Jewish roots and home to a wonderful new
faith in Yeshua Hamashiach, Jesus the Messiah. Somewhere back in my
teen years, I got lost, but somehow, the Lord led me home to Alamosa,
to the ranch Great-Great-Grandfather Gerd built when he came to
America from Germany with his wife, Emily, and his mother, Magda,
during World War II. And my great-uncle, Jürgen, who really considers
himself Amish, though he says he's not a 'joiner', has taken me in and
has taught me much about the Amish already. Indeed, I received a
wonderful Amish Christmas Blessing from Uncle Jürgen, his Amish
housekeeper, Maggie, and my new friend, Johan Eicher, Maggie's son.
We spent Second Christmas at the Eicher farm, and it was the best
Christmas I ever had. And as I find out more about the Amish, and
spend time with the Amish people of Monte Vista, it almost makes me
want to be Amish. But... I have a few things to do before I think about
that.

I want to follow in my grandmother Adina's footsteps as a writer, so I've signed up for some courses in the spring at Adams University in Alamosa—English, Journalism, and History. Uncle Jürgen gave me some good advice and so I'm planning on getting my teaching certificate as a backup, but in my heart, I want to be a storyteller—writing about the Amish in America and Europe, and the history of the Jews in their ancient land. I'm taking a course at an online yeshiva—that's a Jewish school—and I want to study the Torah and the Bible. Uncle Jürgen says that if I study enough, the local Jews will probably accept me as one of them because of my bloodline.

So, I have filled my plate with enough to do for the next while, and it feels like my horizons are opening with a whole new vista I never imagined for my life. Who knows? Perhaps the next time we meet, I will have another story for you... In the meantime, Frohe Weihnachten und ein gutes neues Jahr!

Abigail

ABOUT THE AUTHOR

Patrick E. Craig is an award-winning author with twenty-two published novels. He has won seven CIBA Book Awards, a Selah Award, Two Reader's Favorite Book Awards and a Word Guild Book Award. His work includes three Amish mysteries, six Amish novels, three World War II historical novels with a short story sequel, two anthologies of Amish stories, a standalone novel and a memoir, two YA paranormal books, a redemptive romance, and this new book. He lives in Idaho with his wife, Judy.

PRAISE FOR PATRICK E. CRAIG'S BOOKS

"From the first page of *Jenny's Choice* I felt a tender compassion for Jenny, the young woman in this novel. Her story unfolds with a gentle hand and a lyrical tone that leads to an ending filled with hope. As with the other books in the Apple Creek Dreams series, you'll want to read this book in one sitting. Preferably with a cup of tea."

— ROBIN JONES GUNN, BESTSELLING AUTHOR OF THE GLENBROOKE SERIES AND THE CHRISTY MILLER SERIES

"Patrick Craig's Apple Creek Dreams series is both poetic and sincere. Strong characters who deal with the grief and joy of everyday life make these stories you'll remember long after you reach the last page....*Jenny's Choice* is a tender story of grief, restoration, and grace."

— VANNETTA CHAPMAN, AUTHOR OF THE PEBBLE CREEK SERIES

Patrick Craig writes with an enthusiasm and a passion that is a joy to read. He deals with romance, faith, love, loss, tragedy, and restoration with equal amounts of elegance, grace, clarity, and power. Everyone should pick up *A Quilt For Jenna*, his debut novel in Amish fiction, turn off the phone and computer and TV, and settle in for a good night's read. Craig's book is a blessing.

— MURRAY PURA, AUTHOR OF *THE WINGS OF*

A good storyteller takes a fine story and places it in a setting peppered with enough accurate details to satisfy a native son. Then he peoples it with characters so real we keep thinking we see them walking down the street. A great storyteller takes all that and binds it together with, say, a carefully constructed Rose of Sharon quilt and the wallop of a storm of the century that actually happened. *A Quilt For Jenna* proves Patrick Craig to be a great storyteller.

— **KAY MARSHALL STROM,** AUTHOR OF THE
GRACE IN AFRICA AND *BLESSINGS IN INDIA*
TRILOGIES.

MORE BOOKS BY PATRICK E. CRAIG

A Quilt For Jenna

The Road Home

Jenny's Choice

The Amish Heiress

The Amish Princess

The Mennonite Queen

The Journals of Jenny Hershberger

The Mystery of Ghost Dancer Ranch

The Lost Coast

The Gettysburg Letter

The Amish Menorah and Other Stories

A Christmas Collection

Say Goodbye To The River

Far On The Ringing Plains

The Scepter And The Isle

Men Who Strove With Gods

Beyond The Red Hills

The Drive

The Honor Trail

The Quilt That Knew

The Boy In Blue Denim

3 X 3

When The Hummingbirds Danced In A Honeysuckle Sky

Contact Patrick at pec@patrickecraig.com

Patrick's Website: https://pjpublishing.biz/

Patrick's Amazon Author Page: https://tinyurl.com/y3nwsmgs

THE PORCH SWING MYSTERIES

Book 1—The Quilt That Knew

CHANTICLEER INTERNATIONAL BOOK AWARDS FIRST PLACE WINNER — MYSTERY & MAYHEM FOR COZY AND NOT SO COZY MYSTERIES

- A young girl buried in the woods for forty years...
- A desperate killer loose in the village...
- A mysterious quilt and a golden ring...

Jenny Hershberger returns to Apple Creek, Ohio, the village where she grew up. But this is not a happy homecoming. She's been called upon to solve a horrible crime. But will the killer find her first...

Book 2—The Boy In Blue Denim

CHANTICLEER INTERNATIONAL BOOK AWARDS FIRST PLACE WINNER — MYSTERY & MAYHEM FOR COZY AND NOT SO COZY MYSTERIES

- A young boy murdered in a snowstorm and forgotten...
- A mysterious letter that sets Jenny on the trail...
- Secrets within secrets revealed - nothing is as it seems...

Imagine if Miss Marple were Amish!

Jenny Hershberger returns to Apple Creek, Ohio, called by Detective Elbert Wainwright to help solve another cold case—a young Amish boy murdered in a deadly snowstorm and never identified. But as she digs into the case, she finds so many connections to her own life that the story becomes like a house of mirrors. As Jenny and Bobby Halverson travel from Apple Creek to Shipshewana, to Texas and Colorado, and back to Apple Creek, the trail grows warmer each day. But each step uncovers a new murder... and a new twist. Who is the killer? And who is... THE BOY IN BLUE DENIM?

Book 3—3 X 3

⭐⭐⭐⭐⭐ *Jenny Hershberger is the most unusual amateur sleuth, winning hearts with her courage, compassion, and ability to think outside the box... Reader's Favorite Review*

Jenny Hershberger has returned to Apple Creek, the small Amish Village in Wayne County, Ohio, where she spent her childhood. She purchased her family home and hopes to find peace there.

But then a horrific new mystery comes her way. Three random killings, all marked by the bloody signature of a ruthless serial killer, electrify the little town of Wooster, Ohio. Elbert Wainwright, Jenny's counterpart on the Wooster police force, puts his team to work and quickly hunts down the man they think is responsible—a mentally disabled Vietnam War vet. All the evidence points to Steven Lambright.

But when Elbert calls Jenny and her old friend, retired Sheriff Bobby Halverson, to help, the case against Lambright starts to go south as Jenny discovers there is much more to the story than meets the eye. One by one, Jenny uncovers secrets hidden for forty years, secrets deeply connected to the Amish community. And as she brings them to light, Jenny finds the past can reveal much about the present—in terrifying ways.

THE APPLE CREEK DREAMS SERIES

Book 1—A Quilt For Jenna

Jerusha Springer has spent months making the most beautiful quilt anyone in Apple Creek, Ohio has ever seen, and she knows it is going to take first prize at the Quilt Fair in Dalton. The prize money will be her ticket out of the Amish way of life—away from the memories of Jenna, the daughter she lost a year ago and Reuben, her tormented husband, who has been missing since Jenna's death.

On the way to the fair, Jerusha gets caught in the Storm of The Century. An accident leaves her trapped in her driver's car—and trapped by the memories of her marriage to Reuben and the loss of little Jenna. And then another littler girl enters the story and takes Jerusha's heart captive in a way she hadn't expected. Can this child also be the one to heal Reuben's pain as well?

A beautiful story of loss and redemption.

Book 2—The Road Home

Author Patrick Craig continues the story of Jenny Springer, the child rescued in A Quilt for Jenna, with a story of reconciliation and healing.

Jenny Springer is the local historian for the Amish community in Apple Creek, Ohio. When Jenny was a child, Jerusha Hershberger Springer rescued her from a terrible snowstorm, and when no trace of Jenny's parents could be found, the Springer family adopted her. Since then, the burning desire in Jenny's heart is to find out who she really is.

Then Jenny meets Jonathan Hershberger, a drifter from San Francisco who lands in Apple Creek fleeing a drug deal gone wrong. Intrigued by an *Englischer* with an Amish name, Jenny offers to help him discover his Amish roots. When together they dig into Jonathan's past, Jenny gets serious in her own search for her long-lost parents. And as they travel The Road Home together, Jenny finds the truly surprising answer to her deepest questions, while Jonathan discovers his need for a home, a family, and a relationship with God.

Book 3—*Jenny's Choice*

Jonathan and Jenny Hershberger are happily settled in Paradise, Pennsylvania on the farm Jenny inherited from her grandfather. But when Jonathan disappears in a terrible boating accident, Jenny and her young daughter, Rachel, return home to Apple Creek, Ohio to live with her adoptive parents, Reuben and Jerusha Springer.

As Jenny works through her grief and despair, she discovers she has a gift for writing. A handsome young publisher discovers her work and, after the publication of her first book, Jenny is on the verge of worldly success and possible romance.

Then a conflict arises with the elders of her church, and Jenny must ask herself if she's willing to go outside her faith to pursue her dreams. At the same time, the budding romance is at odds with Jenny's hope that Jonathan might someday be found alive. Jenny must choose and Jenny's Choice leads her to the surprising and heart-warming conclusion of the Apple Creek Dreams series.

THE PARADISE CHRONICLES SERIES

Book 1—The Amish Heiress

Rachel Hershberger's life in Paradise, Pennsylvania is far from happy. Her papa struggles with a terrible event from the past, and his emotional instability has created an irreparable breach between them. Rachel's one desire is to leave the Amish way of life and Paradise forever. Then her prayers are answered. Rachel discovers that the strange, key-shaped birthmark above her heart identifies her as the heiress to a vast fortune left by her *Englischer* grandfather, Robert St. Clair. If Rachel will marry a suitable descendent of the St. Clair family, she will inherit an enormous sum of money. But Rachel does not know that behind the scenes is her long-dead grandfather's sister-in-law, Augusta St. Clair, a vicious woman who will do anything to keep the fortune in her own hands. As the deceptions and intrigues of the St. Clair family bind her in their web, Rachel realizes that she has made a terrible mistake. But has her change of heart come too late?

Book 2—The Amish Princess

Opahtuhwe, the White Deer, is the beautiful daughter of Wingenund, the powerful chief of the Delaware tribe, and a true princess. Everything in her life changes when the renegade known as Scar brings three Amish prisoners to the Delaware camp. Jonathan and Joshua Hershberger are twin brothers that Scar has determined to adopt and teach the Indian way. The third prisoner is Jonas Hershberger, their father, who has been made a slave because he would not defend his family. White Deer is drawn to Jonathan but his hatred of the Indians makes him push her away. Joshua's gentle heart and steadfast refusal to abandon the Amish faith lead White Deer to a life-changing decision, and rejection by her people. In the end, White Deer must choose between the ways of her people and her new-found faith. And complicating it all is her love for the man who can only hate her.

Book 3—The Mennonite Queen

CHANTICLEER INTERNATIONAL BOOK AWARDS SEMI-FINALIST - THE CHAUCER HISTORICAL DIVISION: This is the third book in The Paradise Chronicles series. Isabella, Princess of Poland, is raised to a life of great wealth and leisure in the Polish Royal Court, destined to marry a king. But fate or divine providence intervenes when she meets Johan Hirschberg, a young Anabaptist who works in her father's stable. This chance meeting leads the young couple into a forbidden love. Together they flee Poland and embark on a dangerous journey that brings them, after great peril, to the small parish of a troubled priest named Menno Simons. Catholic Bishop, Franz von Waldek, paid by King Sigismund, Isabella's father to find the princess at all costs, pursues them across Europe. Isabella does not know it, but if von Waldek captures her, she will have to make a choice that will change the course of European history forever.

THE ISLANDS SERIES

Book 1—Far On The Ringing Plains

CHANTICLEER INTERNATIONAL BOOK AWARDS FIRST PLACE WINNER — HEMINGWAY 20TH CENTURY WARTIME FICTION.

FAR ON THE RINGING PLAINS — INSPIRED BY TRUE EVENTS. In the spirit of The Thin Red Line, Hacksaw Ridge, Flags of our Fathers and Pearl Harbor. Realistic. Gritty. Gutsy. Without taking it too far, Craig and Pura take it far enough to bring war home to your heart, mind, and soul. The rough edge of combat is here. And the rough edge of language, human passion, and our flawed humanity. If you can handle the ruggedness and honesty of Saving Private Ryan, 1917 or Dunkirk, you can handle the power and authenticity of ISLANDS: Far on the Ringing Plains. For the beauty and the honor is here too. Just like the Bible, in all its roughness and realism and truthfulness about life, reaching out for God is ever-present in ISLANDS. So are hope and faith and self-sacrifice. Prayer. Christ. Courage. An indomitable spirit. And the best of human nature, triumphing over the worst. Bud Parmalee, Johnny Strange, Billy Martens—three men that had each other's backs and the backs of every Marine in their company and platoon. All three were raised never to fight. All three saw no other choice but to enlist and try to make a difference. All three would never be the same again. Never. And neither would their world. This is their story.

Book 2—The Scepter and The Isle

CHANTICLEER INTERNATIONAL BOOK AWARDS FINALIST — HEMINGWAY 20TH CENTURY WARTIME FICTION

It did not end with Guadalcanal. It did not end with one island. There were more islands... an island with snow-capped peaks, friendly people, blue seas, where Bud found love with his Tongan princess. Where Billy breathed the clean air of mountains where no danger lurked. Where Johnny found a way to drain the hate that drove him mad. They found life again after the death-filled frenzy of Guadalcanal But the God of war was not done with them. More islands sent their siren call from beyond distant horizons and they were cast upon dark shores. Islands with coconut palms, dense green jungle and death. Islands that took more life than they ever gave back. Islands where women killed like men, islands filled with the most brutal soldiers the Japanese Empire could offer. Tarawa. Saipan. Islands that had to be endured. Islands they had to survive. There was no other way to bring the war to an end. There was no other way to get home again.

Book 3—Men Who Strove With Gods

CHANTICLEER INTERNATIONAL BOOK AWARDS FINALIST — HEMINGWAY 20TH CENTURY WARTIME FICTION

 Since 1941 the Marines have fought the Japanese. They met them first on Guadalcanal, a maelstrom of death and fury. Tarawa, Saipan, Okinawa—their friends died beside them, their youth disappeared in a baptism of fire, but they kept on. Johnny, Bud, and Billy went ashore on bloodstained Okinawa hungry for the end of the war. But they knew when the battle ended, they would face their Armageddon on the sacred beaches of Japan.